Credits

Author
John M. Stater

Developer
Bill Webb

Producers
Bill Webb and Charles A. Wright

Editor
Skeeter Green

Layout and Graphic Design
Charles A. Wright

Front Cover Art
MKUltra Studios

Interior Art
MKUltra Studios

Cartography
Robert Altbauer

Special Thanks
Bill Webb would like to thank Bob Bledsaw and Bill Owen for inventing the original hex crawl — the standard in wilderness adventure and a lifetime of fun.

FROG GOD GAMES IS

CEO
Bill Webb

Creative Director: Swords & Wizardry
Matthew J. Finch

Creative Director: Pathfinder
Greg A. Vaughan

V. P. of Marketing & Sales
Rachel Ventura

Art Director
Charles A. Wright

The Maestro
Skeeter Green

FROG GOD GAMES

TOUGH ADVENTURES FOR TOUGH PLAYERS

Table of Contents

Hex Crawl Chronicles

— The Golden Meadows —

By John M. Stater

In a windswept valley of scrub and sand there is a pleasant meadow fed by a bubbling spring. Here a strange people have made their home in a village and fortress of clay that they call Vega. The Vegans do not welcome visitors, and the miles of parched desert that surrounds their home discourages them as well, but still they wander into the valley in search of the silver mines that dot the surrounding hills and mountains. Of course, once these prospectors reach the mountains, they have to worry about the goblin-men and their wicked moonlit rites. Most of these folk begin their adventures in the rough-and-tumble trading port of Sanctum on the Ruddy River, which carries the xenophobes of Halaya down from the north and the war-like golden men up from the south.

The old legends speak of a city that commanded a great empire in these barren lands, a city that shimmered with light, turning the dark of night into the light of day; a city of warriors who patrolled the skies on thundering wyrms; a city where the women possessed the beauty of the nymphs and dressed entirely in precious stones carved out of the mountains. There are no signs of this city now, in the valley of the golden meadows, only the simple fortress-village of the Vegans. The legends also tell of the grand city's fall, of a doom that coursed out of the sky on scintillating wings of fire and laid low men, women, children and beasts. The city was reduced to ash, the valley a sea of burning light. These were the legends found carved on stones in caves by the outcasts of Halaya, who traveled down the river and founded the fishing village of Sanctum. Soon, the village became a trading center between the usually xenophobic Halayans and the golden men of the south, not to mention dwarf caravans that came through secret tunnels from the Pillars of Heaven in the east.

The Golden Meadows of the title actually are rather small, taking up a few hexes in the center of a scrubby desert that broils from late spring to early fall, has a few weeks of nice weather in the early spring and late fall, and then has a mild winter that only occasionally turns frosty. The meadows are watered by vigorous springs, and support a strange, humanoid people called Vegans, named for their fortress-town, Vega. A larger meadow can be found beyond the mountains, and serve as an oasis for caravans traveling from the western lands beyond the Bear Mountains located to the west of the map in this hex crawl.

The desert is interrupted by a central mountain range and barren badlands. The mountains are snow-capped in the winter and fairly well-watered the rest of the year, with intermittent droughts. They support evergreens in the middle elevations, Joshua trees in the low elevations, and are rocky and barren in the high elevations. The mountains are inhabited by goblin-men.

To the east, there is The Lake (as it is termed by the locals, travelers have taken to calling it Sanctuary Lake), surrounded by jagged, red-stoned badlands on all sides. The trading port, Sanctum, sits just to the north of Sanctuary Lake on the Ruddy River. Sanctum holds what passes for human civilization in the region.

The Golden Meadows is a hex-crawl, referring to the hex-shaped units that divide the map. Just as dungeon adventures take place on a gridded map, wilderness adventures can be conducted on a hex map, allowing players the freedom to decide where their characters roam and giving them the thrill of discovering the many places and people that have been placed on the map. This map represents a large area filled with numerous places to discover and explore, and can be used as a campaign area in its own right, or dropped into an existing campaign. Referees can place adventures they have purchased or devised on their own into empty hexes on the map.

Adventures in the Wilderness

The hexes on this map are 6 miles wide from one side to the other. In open country, adventurers should be able to see from one side of the hex to another. In wooded hexes, vision is much more restricted. Random encounters with monsters should be diced for each day and each night, with encounters occurring on the roll of 1–2 on 1d6. The exact monster (or monsters) encountered depends on the terrain through which the adventurers are traveling. Unlike dungeons, in which the monsters on the upper levels are usually less powerful than the monsters on deeper levels, wilderness encounters are quite variable in their challenge, and low level characters face death every time they step out of the confines of civilization. Well-traveled adventurers will discover, however, that settled lands are not as dangerous as the rugged wilderness.

Goblin-Men

The goblin-men are a bit of a misnomer, for they have no actual goblin blood flowing through their veins. In fact, they are mutated remains of the people who once inhabited the valley of the golden meadows. They appear as prune-faced men and women, lanky of limb, slightly hunched, with long fingers and toes that allow them to climb as well as an ape. Their skin is dark bronze in color, their eyes black and their hair, what little they have, lank and black. The goblin-men typically arm themselves with flint-tipped spears and stone axes, much like the Vegans and grimlocks, though they also trade with the kobolds beneath the mountains for metal weapons and armor; about 2 in 6 goblin-men have a metal weapon, 1 in 10 wears ring armor and 1 in 20 wears chainmail.

The goblin-men are hunter-gatherers, living in small bands of 10–20 warriors and their women and children (assume 2.5 non-combatants per warrior). Goblin-men have no chiefs, though most bands have a large male warrior with an extra Hit Dice who bullies the others and keeps the best treasure for himself. Being voracious omnivores, they keep no animals or prisoners longer than their bellies keep from the grumbling. The goblin-men have an innate fear of the shadows (monsters, not absences of light) and shimmering radiances, and avoid them at all costs.

Goblin-Man: HD 1; **AC** 4 [15]; **Atk** weapon (1d6+1); **Move** 12; **Save** 17; **AL** C; **CL/XP** 1/15; **Special**: none.

Vegans

The vegans (no relation to the idea of not eating meat; they enjoy a nice, bloody steak) are a humanoid people who dwell on the golden meadows, herding nimble, blue-black cattle and cultivating fungal gardens (what good is steak without mushrooms!) They are tall (averaging about 7–1/2 feet), thin and hairless, with very small, delicate noses and large eyes that range from topaz to jet. Their chins are narrow and their mouths small. Vegans have alabaster skin that turns a lovely, warm grey in the summer sun, and their fingers are long and delicate. Warriors among them wear coats of scale armor (AC –4 [+4]) that reach to their knees and are kept highly polished. They might carry spear or scimitar and wicker shield or pole arms or light crossbow and scimitar. The Vegans are delighted by music, and will usually regard people who sing and play music much more favorably. They are primarily cattle herders, though they also keep

1 Hex - 6 Miles

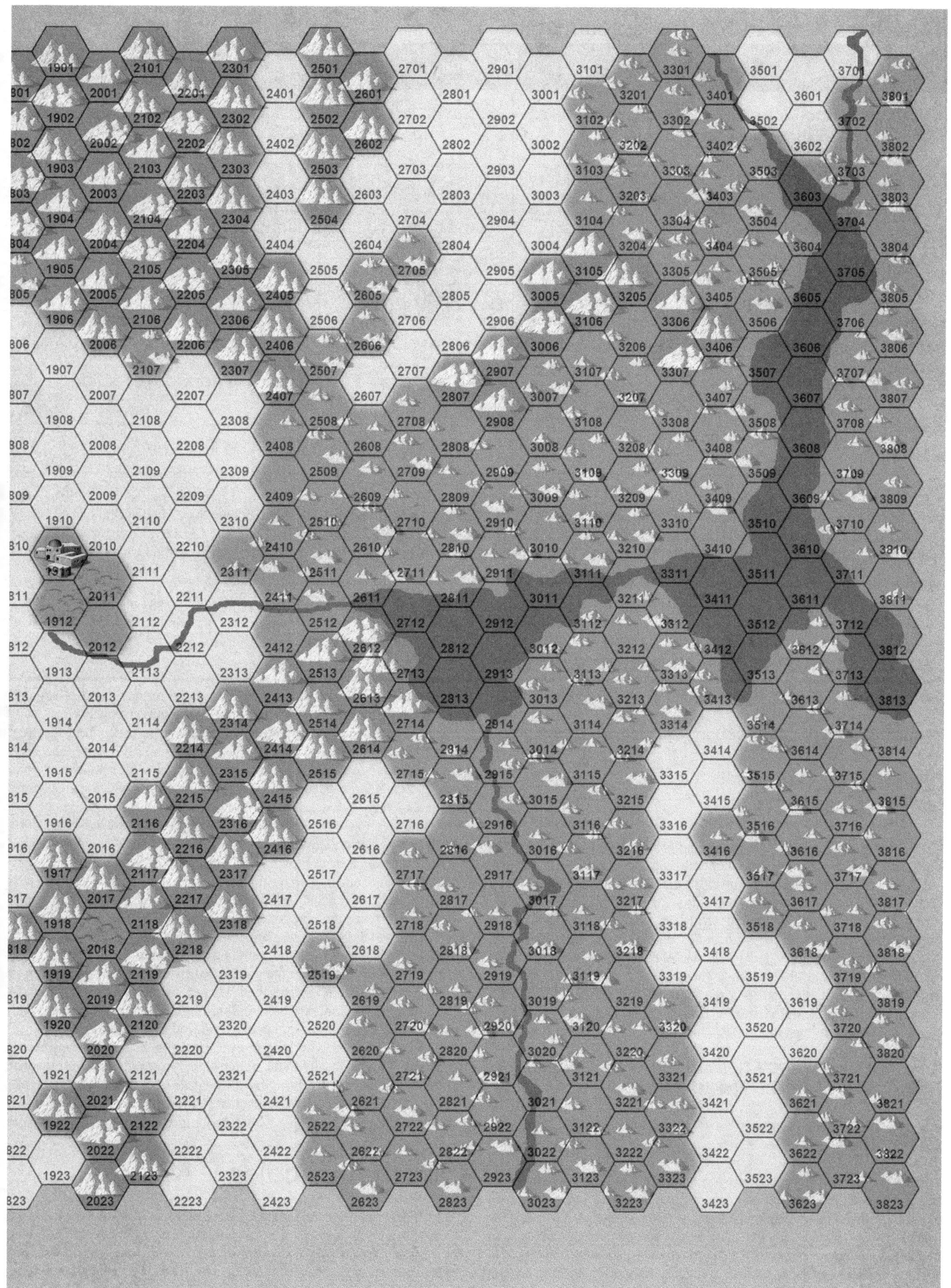

Wilderness Random Monster Encounters

Roll	Badlands	Deserts and Grasslands	Mountains	What Are They Doing?
1	Shadow (1d4)	Bulette (1)	Goblin-Men (2d6)	Arguing Loudly
2	Shadow Mastiff (1d4)	Vegan Hunters** (2d4)	Kobolds (3d6)	Fighting (roll another random encounter)
3	Giant Lizard	Goblin-Man Raiders (2d6)	Bighorn Sheep (1d6)	Fleeing in terror
4	Giant Bats (1d8)	Giant Lizard (1d3)	Prospectors*	Hunting
5	Giant Viper (1d3)	Giant Scorpion (1d4)	Shadow (1d4)	Lurking in ambush
6	Shimmering Radiance*** (1)	Giant Viper (1d3)	Snapping Dragonet*** (1d6)	Lying dead, bodies looted
7	Grimlock (2d6)	Shimmering Radiance*** (1)	Giant Raven (1d6)	Making camp
8	Prospectors*	Ghouls (1d6)	Werebear (1d4)	Marching (random direction)
9	Varghoul*** (1d4)	Camelop*** (2d10)	Archer Tree (1d3)	Reveling
10	Viper Hound*** (1d4)	Giant Raven (1d6)	Wolf (1d8)	Searching for something

* Prospectors are really just bands of adventurers out of Sanctum looking for veins of silver. They consist of 4 to 6 adventurers (1d4+2 levels for each), with bearers equal to the total class levels of the adventurers, and 1d4 men-at-arms per adventurer. 1 in 6 adventurers is a demi-human (roll 1d6: 1–3 Dwarf, 4 Elf, 5–6 Halfling). Roll 1d10 to find a human adventurer's class: 1–3 Fighter (5% chance of paladin); 4–5 Cleric (35% chance of druid), 6 Magic-User; 7–8 Thief (15% chance of assassin or monk); 9–10 Ranger. Men-at-arms usually wear leather armor and are armed with spears and short bows, with 1d20 arrows.

** Vegan hunters carry javelins with atlatls (+1 damage, double range), flint-tipped spears (1d4 damage) and flint knives (1d3 damage). About 1 in 6 vegan hunters carries a normal spear or dagger looted from an outsider. Armor is always leather.

*** Indicates a new monster described at the end of the book.

small gardens of vegetables and fruit trees nearer their complex.

Vegan: HD 1; **AC** 14; **Atk** weapon (1d8); **Move** 12; **Save** 17; **AL** N; **CL/XP** 2/30; **Special:** 1/day—*ESP*.

Grey Travelers

The so-called "Grey Travelers" are smallish humanoids with light grey skin, over-sized heads and large, almond-shaped black eyes … oh heck – they're grey aliens. The greys dwell in the northwest, supposedly in a virtual paradise. They travel in caravans with their tame ankhegs (they appear to be able to communicate with one another), drawing bullet-shaped metal canisters filled with goods manufactured in their realm, as well as a strange, salty red weed that is favored in Sanctum for its use in iron rations and for making a gooey stew. Treat the grey travelers as halflings with darkvision to a range of 60 feet. They are typically encountered in plastic armor (treat as leather armor) and armed with light crossbows and morningstars.

Grey Traveler: HD 1; **AC** 9 [10]; **Atk** weapon (1d6); **Move** 6; **Save** 17; **AL** N; **CL/XP** 1/15 **Special:** none.

Humans

The **Golden Men** were first introduced in *HCC 1 – Valley of the Hawks*, and can be found to the west and south of this hexcrawl. The golden men of the south dwell on a steaming plateau covered by a speckled wood. They wear tall velvet hats, feathered nose rings, wolf-pelt robes, leather foot wrappings and feathered toads. The only southmen encountered in Sanctum are merchants who pedal all manner of fungus, transporting them in baskets hanging from rainbow-colored (blue-grey, rust red and golden brown), nimble-footed cattle. Warriors rarely wear more than long, chainmail hauberks and arm themselves with scimitars and curved daggers.

The golden men (women actually, read on) who come from the west arrive from the fabled desert of glass. The desert men never leave the valley, using their wives and daughters as factotums. They wear head-to-toe white robes and veils and beaded headdresses, the patterns of which indicate their husband's livery. The warriors among them wear coin armor (treat as ring armor; the coins are of ancient mintage and made of nickel and zinc) under their robes, and arm themselves with long swords. They also wear leather girdles from which hang three blades. The warriors spin while they fight, allowing them to attack (in a fashion) with the blades in their hands as well as the blades on their belts. These women never speak, but rather use a sign language that relies on them touching a person with their delicate fingers. These traders of the west drive giant, translucent century worms loaded with the glass goods for which their desert home is famous.

The **Halayans** come from the north, up the Red River. They are men of grim demeanor (one never sees their women, who remain in the safety of their empire in the mountains), dressing in long tunics of black covered by mail haubergeons and metal helms reminiscent of the Japanese jingasa. They arm themselves with long muskets (treat as heavy crossbows) and hand axes. They primarily trade animal skins, salted meat and all manner of vegetables and grains, bringing it down on keel boats. The Halayans believe that women are divine, and must be protected and cherished above all other things.

Other Humanoids

The most commonly encountered humanoids in the Golden Meadows, other than the goblin-men, are the subterranean grimlocks and kobolds. The kobolds are miners and worm-herders, while the grimlocks keep herds of human slaves whose minds have been crushed by their mysterious masters, using them for food and labor. The lake is inhabited by a large

Rumors

When adventurers are seeking information or rumors in a settlement or from the lord of a castle, you can roll a random rumor from the table below. Each rumor is either True ("T") or False ("F") and the hex number associated with the rumor is given in brackets.

Roll	True Rumors	Roll	False Rumors
1	There are few sources of information about the region better than the tree men of the western valley [Hex 0411]	11	The mistress of Vadaskor likes her chin tickled [Hex 0210]
2	A ghostly wind haunts the mountains in the west [Hex 1215]	12	There are several weird statues in the west that come to life under the full moon and can tell the location of a fabulous treasure [Hex 0603]
3	There is a strange ruin hidden in a box canyon to the southwest that supposedly hides a portal to another world [Hex 1219]	13	The goblin-men are frightened of cats
4	Cathedral Rock hides a strange temple [Hex 1312]	14	If you find bleached bones in the desert, beware – they might jump up and attack! [Hex 1518]
5	When the moon is full, one might glimpse strange spirits warring over the desert landscape [Hex 1622]	15	They say that an ancient robber baron hid his booty in a cave of bats [Hex 1702]
6	The red ruins north of Vega are rife with rat men [Hex 1910]	16	Do not fear the Eyes of Zok – they bring glad tidings! [Hex 1816]
7	The old mines one finds in the badlands are often dangerous [Hex 1921]	17	The Vegans delight in human sacrifice [Hex 1911]
8	If you need healing, seek out Guksu, the spirit of the south [Hex 2018]	18	The desert around Vega is poisonous – the sand, the wind – one must drink holy water to stave off the effects
9	Purple worms leave valuable droppings [Hex 2316]	19	If you need healing, seek out Suupadax, the spirit of the north [Hex 2102]
10	The abandoned town in the northern valley is haunted – don't go there without a holy man unless you want to lose your soul [Hex 2904]	20	A coven of witches and warlocks meets secretly in the badlands east of Vega – shun them! [Hex 2510]†

tribe of locathah who dwell in a submerged town and cultivate kelp and herd giant catfish. The locathah themselves resemble catfish, and they have long "whiskers" that carry a slight electric shock.

Encounter Key

0108 Golden Man Caravan from West

A caravan of golden men from the western desert of glass is making its way through this hex to Sanctum. The caravan consists of **seven translucent century worms**, each about 30 feet long and 5 to 7 feet thick. Platforms made of leather, spun glass and wood are strapped to the great beasts. Six of the beasts carry trade goods – mostly glass goods, glass beads and fancy pottery. The seventh worm, located in the middle of the caravan, carries the **factotum**, who wears the beads of her lord, Aphlex, her **four bodyguards** and the worm's driver. The other worms have a driver and **two guards**. The golden men are not averse to traveling with others, though they will not permit foreigners to ride their worms. They are carrying about 300 gp worth of glass goods with a peculiar yellow glaze much favored by the dwarves of the Pillars of Heaven.

Century Worm (7): HD 5; **AC** 7 [12]; **Atk** trample (2d4); **Move** 9; **Save** 12; **AL** N; **CL/XP** 5/240; **Special:** none.

Drivers (7): HD 1; **AC** 6 [13]; **Atk** weapon (1d8); **Move** 12; **Save** 17; **AL** N; **CL/XP** 1/15; **Special:** none.

Guards (12): HD 1; **AC** 6 [13]; **Atk** weapon (1d8); **Move** 12; **Save** 17; **AL** N; **CL/XP** 1/15; **Special:** none.

Bodyguards (4): HD 3; **HP** 10, 14, 9, 11; **AC** 5 [14]; **Atk** weapon (1d8); **Move** 12; **Save** 14; **AL** N; **CL/XP** 3/60; **Special:** Those within 5 feet must save each round or suffer 1d4 points of damage from flaying blades.

Factotum: HD 1d4 hp; **HP** 4; **AC** 8 [11]; **Atk** weapon (1d4); **Move** 12; **Save** 18; **AL** N; **CL/XP** B/10; **Special:** none.

0115 Xa-matutsi

A yawning cave in the western range of mountains is carved to resemble a serpent's head, with glittering spheres of quartz for eyes. Fresh water pours from the serpent's mouth, forming a small rivulet with many waterfalls and pools that flows into the desert and then disappears. The cave is home to **Xa-matutsi**, the western water spirit, who takes the form of an elemental water dragon.

The interior of the cave is composed of blue-green quartz that is highly polished. The stream of water that flows from the cave appears to originate in a large, elevated pool about 30 feet in diameter. Water flows over the sides of this pool to form the river. This is the entrance to Xa-matutsi's lair, and it is guarded by **a large water elemental** that dwells within the pool. The pool is 40 feet deep. At the bottom of the pool there is a small dimension portal in the shape of an ouroboros that leads to a demi-dimension of water (or the Elemental Plane of Water, if you prefer). Not far from the portal dwells Xa-matutsi, in a palace of jade and pearl, attended by naiads and nixies and other water creatures. Xa-matutsi is sometimes invoked by the holy men and women of the region, when they need to access his great wisdom. They must bring valuable offerings to him, most especially objects of jade and pearl.

Xa-matutsi: HD 24; HP 114; AC –2 [21]; Atk bite (2d8) and 2 claws (2d6); Move 0 (fly 15 and swim 36); Save 3; AL N; CL/XP 33/8300; Special: breath weapon (3/day, cone 50' long x 30' wide of superheated water, 14d8 damage, save for half), drench (touch puts out fires, dispels magic fire), magical abilities (1/day—*part water, lower water*), +2 or better weapon to hit, transparency.

Water Elemental (12HD): HP 60; AC 2[17]; Atk strike (3d6); Move 6 (swim 18); Save 3; AL N; CL/XP 12/2000; Special: overturn boats.

0203 Silver Mine

A small, irregular cave here leads into a silver mine. Not far beyond the cave there is a shaft (30 feet deep) that leads into the mine proper, which is populated by a band of **20 goblin-men**. The goblin-men recently killed the human miners who worked the mine with the help of **Tablas**, an agent of Vermes, the chaos cult leader in Sanctum. Tablas is now a captive of the goblin-men, who plan on cooking him in the morning to celebrate their victory. The goblin-men have a treasure of 210 cp, 1,127 sp, 140 gp and a large turquoise worth 800 gp. The silver mine is still active, and is now technically owned by **Yoland**, the orphaned son of the mine's original owner, a miner and adventurer named Rostum. Rostum occupied a smallish brick house in Sanctum, a house now occupied by his son and housekeeper, a crusty old dwarf named **Zgurt**. Zgurt has a peg leg and a glass eye, which he is fond of removing and polishing while telling stories of his old life in the great mountains to the east, the Pillars of Heaven. Zgurt and Yoland do not know Rostum is dead yet, though Zgurt will claim his corn was acting up, and that that is always a sure sign of trouble.

Goblin-Man: HD 1; AC 4 [15]; Atk weapon (1d6+1); Move 12; Save 17; AL C; CL/XP 1/15; Special: none.

Tablas (Thf5): HP 3 (9 normally); AC 9 [10]; Atk short sword (1d6) or dagger (1d4) or shortbow x2 (1d6); Save 11; AL C; CL/XP 4/120; Special: backstab (x3), +2 save vs. traps, read languages, thieveing abilities.
  Thieving Abilities: Climb 89%, Tasks 35%, Hear 4 in 6, Hide 30%, Silent 40%, Locks 30%.
  Equipment: leather armor, short sword, short bow, 20 arrows, 2 daggers, thieves' tools.

Zgurt, dwarf male (Ftr3): HP 13; AC 5 [14]; Atk battle axe (1d8) or hand axe (1d6); Save 12; AL N; CL/XP 3/60, Special: multiple attacks (3) vs. creatures with 1 or fewer HD.
  Equipment: chain mail, battle axe, hand axe.

Yoland: HD1d4; HP 2; AC 9 [10]; Atk weapon (1d4); Save 18; AL N; CL/XP A/5; Special: none.

0210 Vadaskor

This hex holds a large fortress of sandstone and limestone with seven towers, a tall curtain wall (30-ft tall) and a 60-ft. tall keep. Within the curtain wall there is a village of stone houses. Herdsmen graze their goats on the grasses within the wall and without. The wall also holds a roadhouse famous for its pale brews and goat stew flavored with olives and wild onions. The keep is ruled by **Lady Vadaskor**, the Iron Maiden, who commands a corps of **60 women-at-arms** in leather armor armed with spears and sickle-swords and an elite band of **20 chariots**, each with a **driver** and **archer** in scale armor (AC –4 [+4]). Both are armed with long swords and the archer carries a longbow and 20 arrows. Vadaskor guards the valley from incursions from beyond, for the valleys to the west are rife with orcs and goblins.

Vadaskor, human female (Ftr12): HP 74; AC 2 [17]; Atk +2 *flaming longsword* (1d8+2 plus 1d6 fire); Save 4; AL L; CL/XP 12/2000, Special: multiple attacks (12) vs. creatures with 1 or fewer HD.
  Equipment: plate mail, shield, +2 *flaming longsword*.

Woman-at-arms, human female (Ftr3) (60): HP 21; AC 7 [12]; Atk sickle-sword (1d4+1) or spear (1d6); Move 12; Save 12; AL L; CL/XP 3/60. Special: none.
  Equipment: leather armor, sickle-sword, spear.

Chariot driver and archer (Ftr3) (40): HP 18; AC 6 [14]; Atk longsword (1d8) or longbow x2 (1d6); Move 12; Save 12; AL L; CL/XP 3/60. Special: none.
  Equipment: scale armor, longsword, longbow, 20 arrows.

0317 Western Caravan

A **caravan** of the mysterious women from the desert of glass is making its way to Sanctum through this hex. The women are riding (side-saddle, of course) on their massive century worms, which have translucent flesh of a deep rose color. The worms wear coin barding that sparkles and shines in the sun, and have leather packs strapped to them, the packs containing all manner of glassware wrapped in rags. The caravan consists of **seven worms**, each ridden by **one factotum** and **three warriors**. The leader of the caravan is called **Asfa**. She is the headstrong wife of Prince Bubastis, and though quite lovely (one can tell even through the robes and veils – her beauty almost surrounds her like an aura), has little patience for fools.

Century Worm (7): HD 5; AC 7 [12]; Atk trample (2d4); Move 9; Save 12; AL N; CL/XP 5/240; Special: none.

Desert Warriors (21): HD 3; AC 6 [13]; Atk 2 swords (1d6) and 1d3 belt blades (1d6); Move 12; Save 14; AL N; CL/XP 4/120; Special: none.

Desert Factotum (3): HD 1; HP 5, 4x2; AC 8 [11]; Atk dagger (1d4); Move 12; Save 17; AL N; CL/XP 1/15; Special: none.

0411 Joshua Treants

A convocation of **twelve Joshua treants** has gathered in this hex to discuss the last 100 years in the region, and to attempt to find a solution to the problem of the foreign invaders (humans, goblin-men, etc.). It takes them about one hour before they notice outsiders (unless they are attacked), and even then they show little desire to speak with non-druids (who they scold and chide for the liberties taken by the invaders). The treants know about many locations in the region, and might share their knowledge if a service valuable to them (such as clearing out a goblin-man lair in the mountains or burning Sanctum to the ground) is performed first.

Joshua Treants (12): HD 7; AC 2 [17]; Atk 2 strikes (2d6); Move 6; Save 9; AL N; CL/XP 7/600; Special: control trees.

0420 Prismatic Well

In a particularly narrow valley, with tall, sheer walls, there is a man-made well. The well is 200 feet deep, but one could only discover this by falling into it. Prismatic energy, akin to the energy of a prismatic sphere erupts continuously from the well, creating an aurora borealis effect throughout the valley. The light sometimes appears as a dim glow beyond the mountains, but is otherwise hidden by the valley walls. The valley is a pilgrimage site for an astral folk called the prismatic, appearing as "clouds" of energy of ever-shifting colors. These clouds produce a strange hum that becomes higher pitched when they are angry or upset, and takes on a low, throbbing rhythm when they are content. This rhythm generally fills the valley. One can rarely sense the prismatic for the aurora that flows through the valley. There are usually **3d6 prismati** present in the valley.

Prismati: HD 5; AC 1 [18]; Atk touch (2d4 cold, electricity or fire damage); Move 0 (fly 18); Save 12; AL N; CL/XP 10/1400; Special: magical abilities (1/day—*prismatic sphere*), +1 or better weapon to hit, resistance to cold, electricity and fire.

0601 The Margravina

This northern fortress is commanded by a woman who calls herself the **Margravina** (though her old friends in the slums of Crescentium called her Zephira). A born scoundrel and confidence woman, she managed to win this castle in a rather dangerous gambit. The palace is an empty shell keep that has been filled to the brim with wondrous illusions that make it appear as a palace of oriental splendor – rugs, tapestries, furniture inlaid with ivory and draped with silk, vessels of gold, silver and copper, etc. The Margravina has a bodyguard of twelve Fabio-level hunks in loincloths and fur boots and armed with two-handed swords (actually **twelve gnomes** armed with poisoned daggers and wearing leather armor).

The Margravina, Human Female (Thf8): HP 18; **AC** 7 [12]; **Atk** short sword (1d6) or dagger (1d4); **Save** 8; **AL** N; **CL/XP** 7/600; **Special:** backstab (x3), +2 save vs. traps, read languages, thieving abilities.
> **Thieving Abilities:** Climb 92%, Tasks 50%, Hear 5 in 6, Hide 55%, Silent 60%, Locks 55%.
> **Equipment:** leather armor, short sword, daggers (3), thieves' tools, *dust of disappearance.*

Gnome Bodyguards: HD 2; **AC** 7 [12]; **Atk** weapon (1d4); **Move** 12; **Save** 16; **CL/XP** 3/60; **Special:** backstab (x2), magical abilities (1/day—*invisibility, phantasmal force*), surprise on 1–2 on 1d6.

Beneath the stronghold there are limestone caves, in which dwell a tribe of **40 gnomes** — gnarled little men and women with long, white hair. The gnomes are the real power behind the castle. They have been searching in the caves after the philosopher's stone (apparently stowed here a century ago by a band of imp marauders).

Gnomes (40): HD 1; **AC** 8 [11]; **Atk** weapon (1d4); **Move** 12; **Save** 17; **AL** N; **CL/XP** 1/15; **Special:** magical abilities (1/day—*phantasmal force*).

0603 Lord Sivrac

Lord Sivrac was once a celebrated mercenary leader of Sanctum. He was a handsome man, always dangerous with the ladies, who had the misfortune of attracting the attention of **Suress**, a lamia noble who dwelled in a plush cave lair in this hex. When he refused her advances, she used a *wish* (she has a *ring of three wishes* with one wish left) to turn him and his retainers (20 of them) into **stone statues**. The men are still conscious and alive, but unable to communicate save perhaps with a telepath. She sometimes visits the weird statues, who are located about 1 mile away from her cave, bringing along her **two viper hounds** as protection. Her cave holds the following treasures: 3,899 sp, 2,409 gp, a brass pendant depicting a star (worth 45 gp), a bronze sculpture of a cobra worth 90 gp, a pink bottle of jasmine oil worth 25 gp and a large lapis lazuli worth 100 gp.

Viper Hounds (2): HD 4; HP 27, 17; **AC** 4 [15]; **Atk** bite (1d4 + poison); **Move** 18; **Save** 13; **AL** N; **CL/XP** 5/240; **Special:** lethal poison.

Lamia Noble: HD 12; HP 62; **AC** 3 [16]; **Atk** 2 claws (1d6); **Move** 24; **Save** 3; **AL** C; **CL/XP** 15/2,900; **Special:** magical abilities (3/day—*charm person, charm monster, suggestion*), touch drains wisdom (2 points, if fail save by 3 or more you are enslaved).
> **Equipment:** *ring of 3 wishes* (1 wish left).

0608 Goblin-Men

A clan of **20 goblin-men** (5 males, 8 females and 7 children) dwells here in a cave complex in a shady pine vale. One of the caves holds a slimy fungus the goblin-men favor with their raw meat. A thick iron grate blocks entry into the complex, and other passages are likewise blocked. The entry grate is guarded by **a carnivorous ape** chained to the wall. There are two other **carnivorous apes** around the corner on long chains – a nice surprise for intruders. The clan is led by three sorcerous sisters, **Bella**, **Vook** and **Candice**. They keep the others cowed by their powers and their complete lack of mercy.

Goblin-Man (20): HD 1; **AC** 4 [15]; **Atk** weapon (1d6+1); **Move** 12; **Save** 17; **AL** C; **CL/XP** 1/15; **Special:** none.

Carnivorous Ape (3): HD 4; HP 22, 30, 25; **AC** 6[13]; **Atk** 2 hands (1d3) and 1 bite (1d6+1); **Move** 12; **Save** 13; **AL** N; **CL/XP** 4/120; **Special:** hug and rend.

Bella, Vook and Candice, human female (MU3): HP 7 each; **AC** 9 [10]; **Atk** dagger (1d4 + poison) or dart (1d3); **Save** 13; **AL** C; **CL/XP** 2/30; **Special:** +2 vs. spells, spells (2/1).
> **Spells:** 1st—*charm person, magic missile;* 2nd—*phantasmal force.*
> **Equipment:** dagger (poisoned; extra 1d6 points of damage), 5 darts, spellbook.

0714 Shifting Morass

A **large patch of intelligent sand** dwells here. It takes the form of a wandering patch of quicksand, quite unnoticeable except perhaps for a trail of soft sand that lacks any vegetation whatsoever. The patch of quicksand covers roughly a 30-ft. diameter (though it can alter this). Many years ago, a precious stone – a fist-sized topaz – was stolen from the morass and delivered to the lord mayor of Sanctum, who now keeps it on the end of his ceremonial baton. The morass desires the return of this stone (it is like a child who has lost its favorite toy), and is willing to hold people hostage until their friends bring it back. Naturally, it can be difficult to sequester a player character in this way. A Referee might want to instead sequester an NPC, or maybe have the morass extract a solemn vow from a lawful cleric or paladin.

Morass: HD 9; HP 48; **AC** 3 [16]; **Atk** 2 slams (2d6); **Move** 18; **Save** 6; **AL** N; **CL/XP** 11/1700; **Special:** half damage from slashing and piercing weapons, invisible in normal sand, +1 or better weapon to hit.

0901 Heart of Glass

This hex is composed of a vast crater composed entirely of yellowish glass. The entire hex is highly radioactive, forcing travelers to pass a saving throw once per day or lose one level. The crater is inhabited by dozens of **blazing boreworms**, large beasts that burn through the glass, creating small tunnels that crisscross the crater. Within each of these worms there is a strange growth, a sort of glowing yellow nodule. Each one is capable of powering one spell per day of 1st to 4th level (roll 1d4). The stone can cast a total of 30 spells, but each day as a 5% chance of robbing its possessor of one level.

Blazing Boreworm: HD 12; **AC** 4 [15]; **Atk** bite (2d8); **Move** 9 (burrow 6); **Save** 3; **AL** N; **CL/XP** 14/2600; **Special:** immune to fire, swallow whole.

0910 Giant Eagle Aerie

There is a cavern here used as a nesting place for **giant eagles**. They guard the egg of a phoenix that, if placed in a roaring, magical fire, hatches.

Giant Eagle: HD 4; **AC** 7 [12]; **Atk** 2 talons (1d4) or bite (1d8); **Move** 3 (fly 24); **Save** 13; **AL** N; **CL/XP** 4/120; **Special:** none.

1007 Goblin-Men

A clan of **20 goblin-men** dwells here in a cave complex. The entry cave is blocked by a wall of stone with a wooden gate that is always under the guard of four archers; the wall has two arrow slits in it. The goblin-men have a few pelts drying outside their cave complex, and nearby there is a small ravine where they throw their scraps and the bodies of their dead. The goblin-men are ostensibly led by **Vrak**, a large male, but the real power is held by the priestess **Uzha**, who has learned a bit of magic from a mysterious entity that dwells at the bottom of a deep well in the caves. The entity is a lich that was mostly crushed by falling rocks – he whispers his secrets to Uzha in the hopes that she will find a way to free him.

Goblin-Man (20): HD 1; AC 4 [15]; Atk weapon (1d6); Move 12; Save 17; AL C; CL/XP 1/15; Special: none.

Vrak: HD 2; AC 4 [15]; Atk weapon (1d6); Move 12; Save 16; AL C; CL/XP 2/30; Special: none.

Uzha, Goblin-Man Female: HP 4; AC 9 [10]; Atk staff (1d6) or darts x3 (1d3); Save 12; AL C; CL/XP 3/60; Special: +2 vs. spells, spells (3/2).
> **Spells:** 1st—*charm person, magic missile x2*; 2nd—*phantasmal force x2*.
> **Equipment:** staff, 5 darts, spellbook, fetishes and magic powders.

1105 Devil's Foundry

The devil's foundry is a large chamber beneath the earth. The chamber is the workroom of gaggle of **three vrock demons**, which are forging **silent knights** for the eventual war against heaven. The knights are stored in large side chamber, waiting only a single command from a vrock demon to spring into action. In total, there are 20 silent knights completed. The foundry holds about 1 ton of steel and 10 pounds of adamantine (in ingots).

Silent Knight: HD 7; AC 2 [17]; Atk weapon (1d8); Move 9; Save 9; AL N; CL/XP 8/800; Special: silence.

Vrock Demons (3): HD 8; HP 44, 40, 37; AC 1 [18]; Atk beak (1d6) and 2 foreclaws (1d4) and 2 rear claws (1d6); Move 12 (fly 18); Save 8; CL/XP 9/1100; Special: darkness, immune to fire, magic resistance (50%).

1122 Emissary of Lord Zkott

Lord Zkott is an ogre mage who maintains a castle of magically bonded sand in a place known only as the "Valley of Death", a deep valley that is broiling hot and in which the only intelligent life, besides Lord Zkott, are Joshua treants (they abide by the ogre's presence, but do not care for him or his skeletal legions) and igniguanas. Lord Zkott is evil, but he is no fool, and he understands well the value of trade and diplomacy. A small army of forty of his **skeleton** warriors (blackened chainmail, blood red tunics emblazoned with a flaming eye, longsword, longbow, 20 arrows, shield), is escorting his emissary, the succubus **Zrelanna**, to Sanctum to set up various trade agreements with the golden men of the south. She has taken the appearance of a gaunt woman with chalk white skin and stark, white hair in a pageboy cut. She wears black platemail, wields a longsword and lance, and rides a **giant beetle exoskeleton** that has been painted in the livery of Zkott. She has no need for bloodshed, and is willing to travel with others. If attacked, she will allow her soldiers to fight and remain in the background, quitting the field of battle if things go poorly for her forces.

The emissary carries a locked iron box (trapped with a 5 dice fireball that leaves the chest and its contents unharmed) that contains 580 sp and 135 gp. This is meant for gift giving and bribery in Sanctum.

Lord Zkott, Ogre Mage: HD 5+4; HP 33; AC 4 [15]; Atk weapon (1d12); Move 12 (fly 18); Save 12; AL C; CL/XP 7/600; Special: magical abilities, regenerate 1hp/round.

Skeleton: HD 1; AC 4 [15]; Atk weapon or strike (1d8); Move 12; Save 17; AL N; CL/XP 1/15; Special: immune to sleep and charm spells.

Giant Beetle Exoskeleton: HD 5; AC 3 [16]; Atk bite (2d6); Move 6; Save 12; AL N; CL/XP 5/240; Special: immune to turning, immune to non-blunt weapon, unaffected by sleep, hold, and charm.

Zrelanna: HD 6; AC 0 [19]; Atk 2 claws (1d6) or weapon; Move 12 (fly 18); Save 11; AL C; CL/XP 10/1400; Special: immune to electricity and poison, magic resistance (15%), magical abilities (at will—*charm monster, ESP, suggestion, teleport*), +1 or better weapon to hit, speak any language.

1215 Ghost Winds

At the heart of this hex, one might find the bleached bones of a dragon horse. The horse was killed here ages ago by agents of chaos, and its spirit now haunts the hex, whipping up ghostly winds. The winds are unfelt by lawful characters, though they do here a soft music, as though from an unseen flautist. Neutrals feel a balmy breeze that brings tears to their eyes. Chaotic characters feel a hot wind that scours their flesh with blowing sand. They suffer a cumulative 1d6 points of damage per mile traveled in the hex (save for half damage). If the remains of the beast are collected and borne to the tallest mountain in the region **[12.10]**, the spirit is appeased and a reward of 1,000 XP should be given to the characters.

1219 Ant-Lion

At the end of a box canyon filled with thick sand that slows people tremendously there is a portal carved into the wall. The portal has been painted a glossy scarlet, and is decorated with sun symbols. It is the entrance to a small dungeon complex. Beyond the portal there is a large cavern of sandstone walls filled with the same sand. An **ant lion** dwells here, guarding the entrance to the dungeon and taking many adventurers by surprise as they walk in and tumble down its pit. There are only a couple feet between the pit and the walls of the cavern, with three exits on the other side. One is cluttered with bones (due to its being filled with poisonous gas), one descends sharply and smells of rotting flesh and the third is large and uncluttered, and leads eventually to the lair of a **glabrezu demon** who was bound ages ago by a very skilled occultist.

Ant Lion: HD 8; HP 37; AC 2 [17]; Atk bite (2d8); Move 12 (burrow 6); Save 8; AL N; CL/XP 8/800; Special: trap.

[A] This entry chamber is clad in hexagonal golden-brown tiles, each about 2 inches wide. When the door of the room is closed, three seals appear on the other walls. Each seal appears to be made of fired clay,

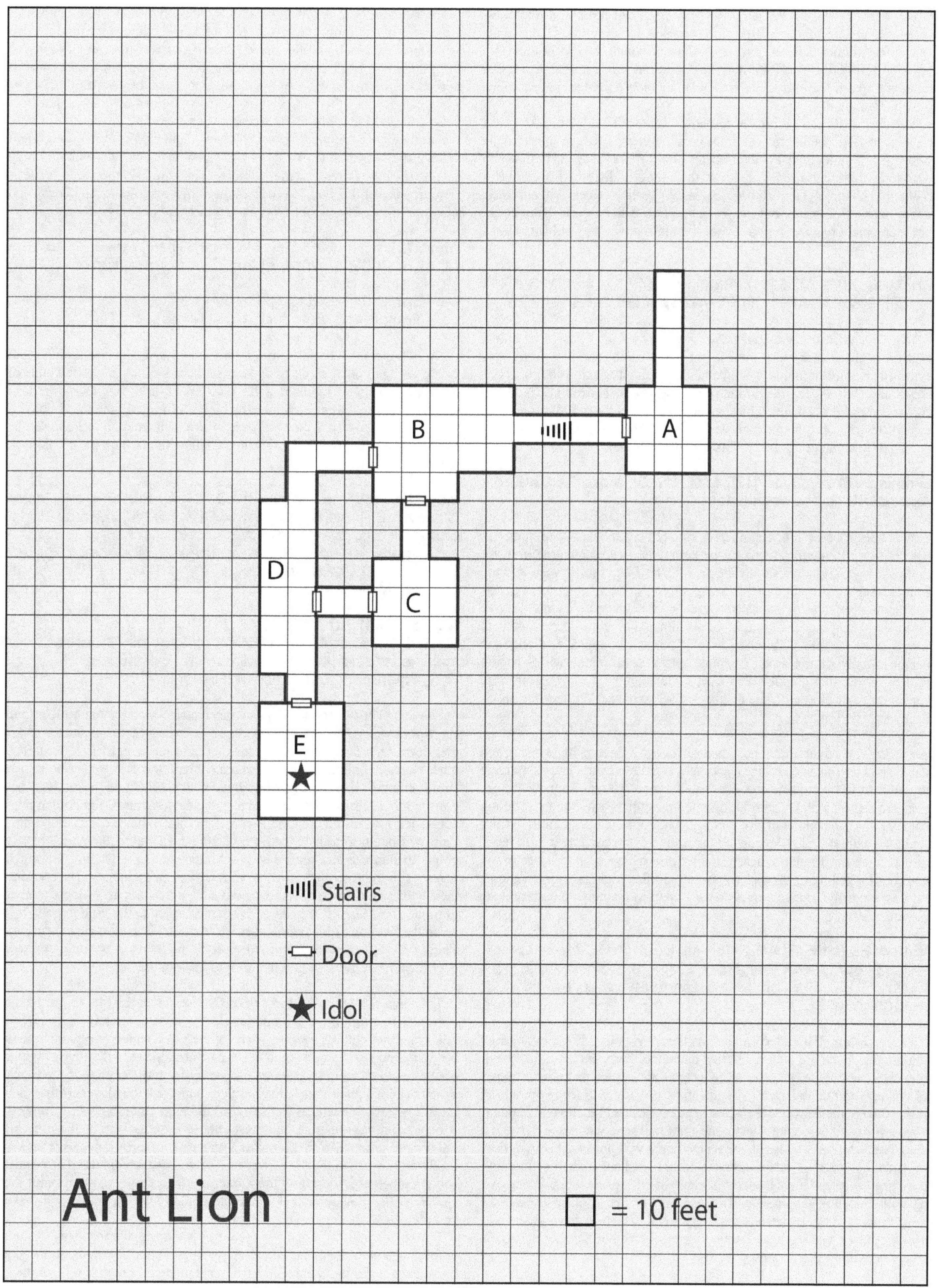

B
A
D
C
E
Stairs
Door
Idol
Ant Lion
= 10 feet

glossy black in color. One depicts a grinning devil holding a pitchfork, another a coiled cobra and the third crossed swords. After these seals appear, the room begins heating up. After one round, people in the room begin suffering damage; 1 point in the first round, 2 in the second, 3 in the third, and so on. The entry door is found to be locked tight (per *wizard lock* by 4th level magic-user).

The clay seals can be broken to permit escape. The devil seal hides a passage to **[B]**. The cobra seal hides poisonous gas (save or die) and the sword seal connects to a subterranean hive of **fire bees**, 2d4 of which will enter the chamber and attack if their hive is disturbed; the hive is home to 3d6 more. The fire bees' royal jelly is like Greek fire, and their honey burns the throat, but can be made into a fiery mead beloved by fire elemental creatures and a few of the more adventurous dwarves and halflings.

Fire Bees: HD 3; **AC** 5 [14]; **Atk** sting (1d4 +1d4 fire); **Move** 9 (fly 30); **Save** 14; **AL** N; **CL/XP** 4/60; **Special:** immune to fire.

[B] This chamber was once the hideaway of an off wizard called Hambroz. He abandoned it long ago, but his harem of 7 very attractive **synthoid women** remains. The synthoids need not eat or drink, but they are bound (via silver torcs around their necks) to this room. The room contains cushions and low tables, a very nice chess set (worth 50 gp) and ten bottles of some manner of synthetic alcohol (very potent, save vs. poison or become drunk and fall asleep in 2d6 turns).

Synthoid: HD 2+2; **AC** 7 [12]; **Atk** fist (1d3); **Move** 12; **Save** 16; **AL** N; **CL/XP** 2/30; **Special:** none.

[C] The floor of this chamber is covered by mosaics depicting six figures from the major arcana of the tarot. The figures pictured here are the Magician, High Priestess, The Devil, The Sun, Temperance and the Hanged Man.

Stepping on an image causes the floor below a person's feet to disappear, dropping them into a pocket dimension where they must deal with a puzzle or threat. To others in the room, it will appear as though the person merely disappeared. Stepping on the same image will a person in a different, though similar, pocket dimension – i.e. if you step on a card, you're dealing with the results solo! The pocket dimensions are as follows:

Devil: The adventurer finds themselves in a cavern of swirling red clouds and terrible screaming. The cavern is cut by several cracks, ranging in width from two to four feet and usually about 10 feet deep. Weird gas rises from these cracks, and falling into one inflicts 1d6 points of falling damage and 1d6 points of fire damage. The room is occupied by a first-category demon called **Vattoo**. Fighting in this room carries with it a 1 in 6 chance per round of nearly falling into a crevice (saving throw to avoid). The ceiling of the cavern is about 20 feet high, allowing Vattoo a little room to fly. The cavern is about 30 feet in diameter and there is no obvious exit.

Vattoo: HD 8; **HP** 48; **AC** 1 [18]; **Atk** beak (1d6), 2 foreclaws (1d4), 2 rear claws (1d6); **Move** 12 (fly 18); **Save** 8; **AL** C; **CL/XP** 9/1100; **Special:** darkness, immune to fire, magic resistance (50%).

Hanged Man: The adventurer finds themselves in a bleak expanse of moorland. There is a single, gnarled black tree here, and from one of its branches there hangs a corpse. The hanged man awakens in the presence of the adventurer, and says, "If you cut me down, I will lead you home." If they do so, the hanged man will stretch his neck and then say, "Lend me your sword and bare your neck to me and I will send you home." (Note, if the adventurer has no sword, the hanged man will produce his own from behind the tree). If the adventurer acquiesces, the hanged man will remove their head and send them back (unharmed) to the mosaic room. Otherwise, he will shrug his shoulders and walk away (or flee if attacked) and the adventurer will be stuck (the hanged man will disappear from view about 100 feet away and cannot be found again). Once the adventurer falls to sleep, he will awaken on the slave ship.

High Priestess: The adventurer finds themselves in a small temple. In the center of the room there is an idol of a winged goddess holding two scimitars, one black and the other white. These swords can be removed from the idol's hands. As soon as the adventurer appears, **two armored priests** step from the walls of the room. One wears black armor, the other white armor, but otherwise they have the same characteristics and both heavy maces. The only difference between them, other than the armor, is that they are immune to physical attacks and magic. While one might believe the swords must be used to destroy them, in fact, one can only destroy them by praying to the idol for salvation or asking for forgiveness, or something of the like. This causes the warrior-priests to back away and sink into the walls and returns the adventurers to the mosaic room.

Priests (2): HD 3; **AC** 3 [16]; **Atk** mace (1d6); **Move** 12; **Save** 14; **AL** N; **CL/XP** 4/120; **Special:** +2 vs. paralyzation and petrification, spells (2).
    Spells: 1st—*cause light wounds* x2.
    Equipment: plate mail, heavy mace.

The Magician: The adventurer finds themselves in a circular room facing an aged **elf** dressed as a magician and holding a gnarled staff of white pine. This elf fights as a 4th level magic-user, but should he take damage, he transforms into a 4th level fighter in plate mail and holding shield and longsword. Likewise, if the warrior incarnation is damaged, he turns back into the magician. One must defeat him in both incarnations to escape this room.

Magician (MU4): HD 4; **HP** 13; **AC** 9 [10]; **Atk** staff (1d4); **Move** 12; **Save** 13 (11 vs. magic); **AL** N; **CL/XP** 5/240; **Special:** elf abilities, +2 vs. spells, spells (3/2)
    Spells: 1st—*charm person, magic missile, shield;* 2nd—*invisibility, mirror image.*
    Equipment: staff

Warrior (FTR4): HD 4; **HP** 26; **AC** 2 [17]; **Atk** longsword (1d8+1); **Move** 9; **Save** 13; **AL** N; **CL/XP** 4/120; **Special:** elf abilities, multiple attacks (4) vs. creatures with 1 or fewer HD.
    Equipment: plate mail, shield, longsword.

The Sun: The adventurer finds themselves in a room about 10 feet long and 6 feet wide. There are two pools here, each 3 feet in diameter and 3 feet deep. One is located on the ceiling, and has a golden bottom. The other has a silver bottom and is located on the floor. The golden-bottomed pool is empty, while the silver-bottomed pool is filled with water. Both are polished to a mirror-sheen. As soon as the person enters, the golden pool begins to glow, filling the room with bright light. After the first round, this light will begin to sear the skin; each round, the adventurer suffers 1d4 points of damage and must save vs. blindness. If the person fails three saves vs. blindness, they will be struck blind permanently. By pressing their body against one of the narrow walls, a person causes the chamber to rotate. This takes 3 rounds, and when completed, the golden pool will be on the floor and filled with water while the silver pool is on the ceiling. The light will cease, the room will become perfectly dark and a moment later the adventurer will find themselves back in the mosaic room.

Temperance: The adventurer finds themselves in a white room. In the center of the room there is a minute-glass with sand already beginning to fall. On either end of the narrow room, there is a statue of a woman, one blue and one red. Each woman has her hands cupped, with a glowing orb floating above them. Spikes are descending from the ceiling of the room. When the encounter begins, the Referee should ask the players (other than the one who's character is in the room) to begin counting down from 60. It may seem obvious that one must choose to touch one or the other of the orbs to escape. In fact, touching either of the orbs causes the spikes to shoot down suddenly, skewering the trapped character. They must show temperance and allow the minute-glass to empty. At that point the spikes will stop about 2 feet above the ground and the person will have completed the challenge.

If the challenge is met and overcome, the person appears back in the room holding a 2-inch diameter sphere of swirling colors. By concentrating, a person can use this stone to shift from one plane or dimension to another.

This is a one-way trip – the stone disappears after use. If a person fails, they awake (even if they were seemingly killed) on an extra-planar slave ship of the enigmatic **kith-yin** coursing through the Astral Plane. Kith-yin look like emaciated elves (they are, in fact related, and are sometimes called astral elves). The ship is about 100 feet long and has a crew of 12 kith-yin. It is commanded by **Captain Okros**. Other adventurers who fail will also be held in the ship, chained to the bulkhead.

Kith-yin (11): HD 4; **AC** 3 [16]; **Atk** silver sword (1d6+1); **Move** 12; **Save** 13; **AL** N; **CL/XP** 5/240; **Special:** magical abilities (at will—*ESP*), psychic blast (1/day; save or suffer 1d4 points of intelligence damage and 1d6 points of hit point damage from pain, intelligence returns 1 point/day).
    Equipment: silver chain mail, silver longsword.

Captain Okros, Kith-Yin Male: HD 4; **HP** 21; **AC** 3 [16]; **Atk** silver sword (1d6+1); **Move** 12; **Save** 13; **AL** N; **CL/XP** 5/240; **Special:** magical abilities (at will—*ESP*), cast spells as 5th level magic-user, psychic blast (1/day; save or suffer 1d4 points of intelligence damage and 1d6 points of hit point damage from pain, intelligence returns 1 point/day), spells (4/2/1).
    Spells: 1st—*charm person, magic missile x2, shield*; 2nd—*invisibility, mirror image*; 3rd—*fireball*.
    Equipment: silver chain mail, silver longsword.

[D] This room is really a hallway. It leads to the chamber of the glabrezu demon mentioned above. The hallway's walls, ceiling and floor are pocked with holes that give out gouts of steam at what first seem to be random intervals. In fact, this steam follows a rhythm. If adventurers pause for a bit, they will learn that the rhythm is "boom-boom-pop-boom-pop-pop-boom-boom-boom-pop". The pops represent when it is safe to walk, with each stride being 5 feet. The booms are the explosions of steam. As Referee, you can repeat the rhythm for each minute they stand watching, but each minute spent here has a 1 in 6 chance of summoning the attention of **a water elemental**. To cross the hallway, a player must repeat the rhythm. Any bit they get incorrect deals 1d6 points of damage and forces them to deduct their damage and then begin from the point at which they stopped.

Water Elemental (8HD): HP 44; **AC** 2[17]; **Atk** strike (3d6); **Move** 6 (swim 18); **Save** 8; **AL** N; **CL/XP** 8/800; **Special:** overturn boats.

[E] Here, then, is the final room, the prison of the glabrezu demon **Parthok the Despoiler**. When one enters this rather rough chamber, they must first be struck by the golden idol that dominates it – a depiction of a man, seated in the lotus position, in deep meditation, a sapphire embedded in his forehead as a "third eye". The idol appears to be made of wood covered by gold leaf, and rests upon a pedestal. Pedestal and idol are surrounded by a magic circle of silver dust anchored by five precious stones – bloodstones worth 200 gp each. The idol is, of course, not an idol, but rather an illusion thrown up by the glabrezu. Here he waits anyone foolish enough to step over the magic circle or greedy enough to steal one of the bloodstones and release him to work his evil.

Parthok: HD 10; **HP** 52; **AC** –3 [22]; **Atk** 2 pincers (2d6), 2 claws (1d3) and bite (1d4+1); **Move** 9; **Save** 5; **AL** C; **CL/XP** 11/1700; **Special:** demonic magical powers, magic resistance (60%).

1311 Goblin-Men

A clan of **15 goblin-men** occupies what appears to have been a large inn in ancient times. The inn has two stories, with a large common room and stairs from there that lead to the upper floor of rooms (there are about 20 rooms on the top floor and 20 on the bottom floor. The rooms are dank and small, and most are empty. Those that are occupied are either used as living quarters for the goblin-men or kennels for their hounds. One room is used as an armory, and contains seven shields, fourteen short bows, 150 arrows and ten spears. Off the common room there is an old taproom (no spirits remain) as well as a large room used by the **clan's biggest male** and his retinue of thugs.

Goblin-Man (15): HD 1; **AC** 4 [15]; **Atk** weapon (1d6+1); **Move** 12; **Save** 17; **AL** C; **CL/XP** 1/15; **Special:** none.

Skork: HD 3; **HP** 10; **AC** 4 [15]; **Atk** dagger (1d4 + poison) or dagger (1d4) or shortbow x2 (1d6); **Move** 12; **Save** 14; **AL** C; **CL/XP** 4/120; **Special:** backstab (x2), disguise, poison, thieving abilities.
    Thieving Abilities: Climb 85%, Tasks 15%, Hear 3 in 6, Hide 10%, Silent 20%, Locks 10%.
    Equipment: leather armor, shield, dagger (lethal poison), 2 daggers, short bow, 20 arrows.

1312 Cathedral Rock

Cathedral rock is a barren rock face with a small temple carved into it about 200 feet above the ground and 40 feet below the top. The temple is about 20 feet long, 20 feet wide and 20 feet high. The floor is actually set four feet below the entryway, and is filled 4 feet deep with skulls and other bones. In the middle of the temple there is a pedestal (4 feet high) on top of which is set an idol depicting a deity with three torsos and heads atop six legs. There are hundreds of adamantine scarabs set into the walls. These are the temple guardians; they form a **swarm** and attack whenever a magical creature or spellcaster enters the chamber, for this temple is dedicated to a now forgotten deity of anti-magic. The swarm can attack all creatures within a 10-ft. radius.

Scarab Swarm: HD 8; **HP** 37; **AC** 1 [18]; **Atk** swarm (1d8); **Move** 12 (fly 18); **Save** 8; **AL** N; **CL/XP** 10/1400; **Special:** creatures within the swarm must pass a saving throw or be stunned for 1 round or panic and flee (50% chance of either), half damage from bludgeoning weapons, minimum damage from slashing and piercing weapons.

The pedestal of the idol contains a secret door that grants access to a spiral stair that delves into the heart of Cathedral Rock, wherein there is a tomb of a high priest and his coterie of witch hunters. The tomb is protected by various anti-magic traps and mechanical monsters. The priest is interred in a lead vault, for he actually survives as a being of pure radioactive energy.

1403 Lonely Basilica

A strange basilica of limestone carved with bas-reliefs of dinosaurs sits here in the midst of the desert. The basilica has doors of thick glass, and windows of a similar material. The strange temple contains a number of sculptures that appear to be dinosaur-headed men wearing togas. A large idol sits at the end of the nave, a pulsating cube of spiraling colors. In the presence of the cube, adventurers feel themselves grow dizzy, and the spiraling colors move from the cube into the rest of the room. The statues appear to twist and melt, as do the walls, and for a moment, gravity is cancelled. All of a sudden, the effect stops and the adventurers come to their senses in a basilica that is now submerged. Outside the glass windows and doors, one sees a shallow sea in which dwell all manner of prehistoric shelled creatures and cunning ichthyosaurs, not to mention the original inhabitants of the land, crabmen and starfish-people, who waged great and terrible wars with one another. The submerged temple can be escaped by touching the cube, which teleports people to one of the mountain hexes in the region, which poke above the sea level as islands. How adventurers get back to their own time (or if they ever get back) is a matter for them to figure out.

1518 Bleached Bones

A bleached skeleton pokes up from the sand here; just the skull, shoulder blades and a single arm. If one unburies it, they discover it was a centaur adventurer, its equine bits still clad in mail barding. Underneath this barding the centaur kept a silver mirror wrapped in thick cotton wadding.

1606 Fortress of Tears

A ramshackle fortress composed of some manner of strange stone (concrete, it turns out) has been erected here to guard the way to the north. Carvings in the fortress suggest it was the work of Halayans. There are thirty statues strewn about the castle, all of them depicting lovely men and women in togas. A slow trickle of tears falls from the eyes of the statues. If collected and rarified by a night bathed in moonlight, the tears act as magic potions. It takes 30 minutes to collect enough tears to make a potion, and a magic-user has a percentage chance equal to his or her level x2 to properly prepare the tears under the moonlight.

Roll	Statue	Potion
1	Mustachioed Warrior	heroism
2	Debauched Lord	healing
3	Demure Lady	invisibility
4	Wizened Sage	clairaudience
5	Wanton Woman	resistance
6	Defeated Barbarian	giant strength

The fortress is home to a nest of **giant marble snakes**, who dwell in a series of caverns beneath the fortress that are connected (via a 4-ft. diameter hole) to the cellar, where one can also find mason's tools and a wooden chest holding 5 pounds of colored, ground glass. The snakes come out to hunt at night or when they hear people stirring above. Their caverns are winding and confusing, and permit access, via a long, narrow cleft in the rock, to the Red River several miles away.

Giant Marble Snake: HD 9; AC 1 [18]; **Atk** bite (2d4 + paralysis for 1d6 days); **Move** 12; **Save** 6; **AL** N; **CL/XP** 12/2000; **Special:** immune to paralysis and petrification, surprise on 1–3 on 1d6 in rocky areas.

1622 Moonlit War

When this hex is illuminated by a full moon, one sees ghostly figures fighting a great battle. The figures are some sort of **toad-like humanoids** in banded armor and wielding crescent-headed axes and barbed lances. One side of this battle fights for the forces of Law, and wear yellow tunics, while the other fights for Chaos, and wears white tunics. Two of the toad men are capable of sensing onlookers. Both are **priests**, and both attempt to lure other priests and paladins (in the case of the toad warriors of Law) to their aid. This can be accomplished by swallowing a small marble presented by one of these ghostly toad clerics. If the pebble is taken and swallowed, the cleric or paladin is thrust through dimensions into the battle, appearing now to others as a ghostly figure as well. The battle is an eternal one that is raging on grey, luminous dunes of the Moon. All told, there are 500 warriors on either side, and their ability to regenerate keeps them in the battle. Either side will direct helpers to undertake a special mission into the Sea of Tranquility in search of the brooding Moon King, who might sway the battle one way or the other.

Toad Warrior: HD 3; AC 3 [16]; **Atk** weapon (1d8); **Move** 20; **Save** 14; **AL** L or C; **CL/XP** 6/400; **Special:** hop up to 40 feet as a charge attack, immune to cold, regenerate 3 hp/round.

Toad Priests: HD 6; HP 16 each; AC 4 [15]; **Atk** warhammer (1d4+1); **Save** 10; **AL** L or C; **CL/XP** 7/600; **Special:** banish undead, hop up to 40 feet as a charge attack (20 feet in armor), immune to cold, +2 vs. paralysis and poison, regenerate 3 hp/rd, spells (2/2/1/1).
 Spells: 1st—*cure light wounds* x2; 2nd—*bless, hold person*; 3rd—*prayer*; 4th—*cause serious wounds*.
 Equipment: Chain mail, shield, warhammer, holy or unholy symbol.

1702 Bat Caves

A valley here is screened by a thick copse of pines. Beyond the pines, the valley extends about 5 miles, with sandstone walls and a valley floor that has been carved into a sort of maze with low walls. The valley walls are pocked with caves in which dwell hundreds of **giant bats**. As night falls, the bats explode from these caves; any group of travelers in the maze are assaulted by 1d4 giant bats each round for about 10 rounds. If they are near death, the bats might continue their assault to feed on them. One of the bat caves (there are 30) contains the skeleton of a magic-user in robes of cloth-of-gold (worth 50 gp if cleaned of guano) that hide an ivory scroll case (worth 30 gp) in which there is a *scroll of wish*.

Giant Bat: HD 4; AC 7 [12]; **Atk** bite (1d10); **Move** 4 (fly 18); **Save** 13; **AL** N; **CL/XP** 4/120; **Special:** 10% chance of disease.

1816 Eyes of Zok

The barren landscape here is made significantly more interesting by the presence of two metal orbs that orbit one another about 40 feet above the ground. One orb is rubinescent and gives off a reddish aurora that sears the flesh (save each minute or suffer 1d4 points of damage). The other orb is blue in color and produces a white aura that is blinding and which implants suicidal thoughts into people's minds (save once or become suicidal). The grey travelers worship these orbs, but do not know their origin. They say they can communicate with them, receiving visions of their ancestral homeland. They have constructed a small shrine here, most of it underground. Above ground, one finds a courtyard of black brick and a small steel dome. One climbs into the dome (actually a sphere) by a trapdoor. Once inside, the sphere rotates and one can climb back out the trapdoor and into the shrine.

The shrine is clad in black stone. There are two orbs embedded in opposite walls, one red and one blue. They can be removed by a person with a combined wisdom, intelligence and charisma of 40 or more. The orbs cannot be forced together, but they can be spun around one another. When this is done, all within the shrine are teleported into either one of the large orbs above ground.

The orbs are hollow, each one about 15 feet in diameter. Each one is guarded by **a mercury ooze**. The red orb contains a small, red, metallic cube that, when zapped with any amount of electricity, unfolds into a wall of metal and shifting force fields that are as dangerous as a *blade barrier* spell. The blue orb holds a crystalline scepter called an ethereal regulator. Also activated by electricity, it creates a 30-ft. diameter field that repulses ethereal beings and which can generate 1d6 magic missiles each round against ethereal beings.

Mercury Ooze: HD 5; HP 29; AC 7 [12]; **Atk** strike (2d4 + mercury poisoning); **Move** 12 (climb 9); **Save** 12; **AL** N; **CL/XP** 6/400; **Special:** poison (drain 1 point of constitution and dexterity; 1 week later must save or be struck by insanity).

1910 Red Brick Ruins

There is a ruin here of large, red bricks, piled high into many oddly shaped piles. Each of the piles has a secret door (difficult even for elves to find) that can only be opened by knocking on the correct brick (1 in 10 chance). Three incorrect knocks in a row seals the door tight for 6 days and 6 nights. There are 12 such piles, and all of them lead to a weird, subterranean maze of the red brick, a maze inhabited by **ratlings** and their ratty kin, including a nobility of **wererats**. The rat king, **Scabadar**, is dashing (for a rat). He wears a golden crown encrusted with jewels (worth 2,500 gp) and carries a scimitar. His consort, **Zimba the White**, is an albino female wererat with magical abilities. Scabadar and Zimba command a small army of rats and ratlings. They spend their days and nights plundering the deeper depths of gold and jewels, the remnants of a dwarven mine from elder days. The dwarves sealed many fell beasts here to guard their vaults. The ratlings have avoided these vaults, but would be happy to send adventurers in to plunder them for them.

Ratling: HD 1; **AC** 9 [10]; **Atk** bite (1d6+poison) or weapon; **Save** 17; **Move** 12; **AL** C; **CL/XP** 2/30; **Special:** diseased bite.

Zimba: HD 3; **HP** 12; **AC** 6 [13]; **Atk** bite (1d3) or weapon (1d6); **Move** 12; **Save** 14; **AL** C; **CL/XP** 5/240; **Special:** cast spells as 6th level magic-user, control rats, lycanthropy, surprise, spells (4/2/2).
> **Spells:** 1st—*charm person x2, magic missile x2*; 2nd—*mirror image x2*; 3rd—*hold person x2*.

Scabadar: HD 4; **HP** 16; **AC** 9 [10]; **Atk** bite (1d6 + poison) or weapon; **Save** 13; **Move** 12; **AL** C; **CL/XP** 5/240; **Special:** diseased bite.

1911 Vega

Vega is a large village located on the golden meadows. Inhabited by a strange people called **Vegans**, it is surrounded by 12-ft. tall wall of large caliche blocks. Within the walls, the land is raised about 8 feet above the level of the surrounding grasslands. The village contains about 20 acres, most of which is grazed by the cattle of the Vegans. At the northern end of the village there is a conglomeration of stone buildings that are all connected with one another. The edges of the roofs are studded with spikes. Rope ladders lead up to the roof, where the only entrances to the complex are located. Vegan warriors always patrol these roofs, which range from 10 to 20 feet in height. In the center of the complex, the Vegans keep a temple to their god, which looks like a four-armed Vegan, two hands pressed together in prayer, the other two holding scimitars. This is Meshta, the Vegan's androgynous god of love and war (an Earthling that has been drawn into Namera through a portal – perhaps in an amusement park – would swear it was a statue of David Bowie). The Vegans gather here to pray and meditate, and to blindly drop marbles into bowls (white and black marble) to make decisions for the tribe.

Vegan: HD 1; **AC** 14; **Atk** weapon (1d8); **Move** 12; **Save** 17; **AL** N; **CL/XP** 2/30; **Special:** 1/day—*ESP*.

1912 Black Pyramid

A pyramid of black glass rises about 30 feet above the surface of the land here. It has been broken into in one spot, but is otherwise intact (the glass does not break easily). Inside, one finds a small chamber filled with sand with four doors that lead into shafts that seem, from the angle, to run down the sides of the pyramid, which obviously extends more than 300 feet beneath the ground above. The walls of the pyramid were once lined with thousands of small chambers – probably used for burials or burial items – that are now used by a large tribe of bat-folk. The inside of the pyramid is a great atrium that has been turned into a sort of temple dedicated to Fortuna, the goddess of luck and fate, who is represented here by a large idol in the Egyptian style. At her feet there is an idol of some exotic, dark wood covered by a green cloth marked with mystic symbols in a sort of grid of three columns and twelve rows. A wheel of fortune sits at the end of this altar, and the **bat-folk** use it decide the fate of those who fall into their clutches. The person is permitted to choose one of the 36 squares on the altar. The wheel is spun and the if the sacrificial victim's number comes up, they are permitted to leave with the blessing of the **high priest (Skirree**, an aged bat-woman in a tall, beaded headdress). Those who fail at this test of fortune are dropped into a pit, where they fall 20 feet into a series of catacombs. The lich **Vazgar** dwells in these catacombs, and seeks a mate in the form of an elven female. He has been

crafting an army of iron cobras in these catacombs and plans on using them and his bat-folk to conquer the Vegans and eventually establish a great kingdom for himself, which his mate as the public queen. Vazgar has a treasure of 1,123 sp, 2,285 gp and five pounds of rare incense worth 200 gp per pound.

Bat-folk: HD 1; **AC** 9 [10]; **Atk** bite (1d6) or weapon; **Save** 17; **AL** C; **Move** 12 (fly 21); **CL/XP** 1/15; **Special:** none.

Skirree, bat-folk female: HP 14; **AC** 7 [12]; **Atk** bite (1d6) or weapon (1d6); **Save** 11; **AL** C; **CL/XP** 5/240; **Special:** +2 vs. paralysis and poison, banish undead, spells (2/2).
> **Spells:** 1st—*cure light wounds, protection from good*; 2nd—*hold person x2*.
> **Equipment:** leather armor, heavy mace, throwing hammer, holy symbol.

Vazgar: HD 12; **HP** 50; **AC** 0 [19]; **Atk** touch (1d10 + automatic paralysis); **Move** 6; **Save** 3; **AL** C; **CL/XP** 15/2900; **Special:** appearance causes paralytic fear, touch causes automatic paralysis, spells (4/4/4/4/4/1).
> **Spells:** 1st—*charm person, light, magic missile x2*; 2nd—*detect invisibility, ESP, mirror image, web*; 3rd—*dispel magic, fireball, hold person x2*; 4th—*charm monster x2, dimension door, wall of fire*; 5th—*animate dead, contact other plane, magic jar, teleport*; 6th—*invisible stalker*.

1921 Slag Heaps

At the base of a cliff there is an old mine. A slope extends from the mine entrance about 200 feet at a 35-degrree angle, and this slope is covered by a number of old slag heaps and the remnants of earthen ovens. The mine is currently inhabited by an **aurumvorax**, which has been left to guard a jade idol of an angel. The idol was hidden here by Halayan outcasts, who intended to return for it in the future, that they might place it in a church. Unfortunately, they were wiped out by grimlocks, and those who remain now labor in their slave pits. The idol weighs about 200 pounds and is worth 3,000 gp.

Aurumvorax: HD 12; **HP** 59; **AC** 0 [19]; **Atk** bite (1d8); **Move** 12 (burrow 3); **Save** 3; **AL** N; **CL/XP** 13/2300; **Special:** immunity to poison, rake with claws, resistance to fire (50%), surprise on 1–2 on 1d6.

2004 Dwarf Prospectors

A party of **20 dwarves** has set up camp next to a small rivulet that flows from the mountains here, eventually flowing underground and re-emerging in the springs of the Vegans. The dwarves are panning for silver, and, if they do well, plan on returning in greater numbers that they may challenge the goblin-men of the mountains and establish a fortified mine. The leader of the band is a dwarf lord named **Karack**. He is accompanied by his erstwhile comrade **Bolgum**. The rest are dwarf warriors armed with battleaxes and ring armor, not to mention picks, hammers and other mining tools. The group has enough food here (iron rations) for 20 more days, and plans to plan another 5 and then head back for their home in the great mountains to the east, near the homeland of the Halayans. They currently have 50 pounds of silver ore to show for their efforts, and about 10 goblin-man heads to decorate their shields.

Dwarf: HD 1; **AC** 4 [15]; **Atk** weapon (1d8); **Move** 6; **Save** 17; **AL** L; **CL/XP** 1/15; **Special:** detect attributes of stonework.
> **Equipment:** ring armor, battle axe, mining tools.

Karack, dwarf male (Ftr7): HP 34; **AC** 4 [15]; **Atk** +1 *warhammer* (1d4+2) or silver dagger (1d4) or light crossbow (1d4+1); **Save** 8; **AL** N; **CL/XP** 7/600, **Special:** multiple attacks (7) vs. creatures with 1 or fewer HD.
> **Equipment:** chain mail, shield, +1 *warhammer*, silver dagger, light crossbow, 20 bolts.

Bolgum, dwarf male (Ftr4/Thf5): HP 18; AC 6 [13]; **Atk** dagger (1d4) or handaxe (1d6) or throwing hammer (1d4); **Save** 11; **AL** N; **CL/XP** 7/600, **Special:** backstab (x2), multiple attacks (3) vs. creatures with 1 or fewer HD, +2 save vs. traps, thieving abilities.

> **Thieving Abilities:** Climb 89%, Tasks 35%, Hear 4 in 6, Hide 30%, Silent 40%, Locks 30%.
> **Equipment:** leather armor, three daggers, hand axe, throwing hammer, *ring protection +1*.

2011 Hidden Library

The remains of a library of the ancients are hidden beneath the ground here. A small copse of cottonwood trees obscures a hollow that was once a stairwell. At the bottom of this stairwell, one might note two metal doors that have been forced open by desert sand. The sand spills into a concrete walkway which leads to a number of rooms of various sizes. Many of these rooms have metal shelves and on these shelves one has a small chance of finding the remnants of books and tomes from ancient days, in the strange alphabet of the ancients. There are two dozen rooms here, and each room has a 1 in 10 chance of containing 1d8 ancient books that have not completely disintegrated over time. There is a 1% chance that any one of these books will contain 1d4 magic-user spells (roll 1d4 for level). Otherwise, they would be valuable to collectors. The ancient library is now home to **1d12 giant vipers**.

Giant Viper: HD 4; AC 5 [14]; **Atk** bite (1d3 + poison); **Move** 12; **Save** 13; **AL** N; **CL/XP** 6/400; **Special:** lethal poison.

2015 The Old Manor

In the southern reaches of the main valley, a large building composed of sandstone bears witness to the wealth that must once have filled this valley. The building is constructed upon a small rise with steep sides. It has a flat roof and is built in three circular sections that surround a large courtyard of white stone. The courtyard holds a pool (empty) and is cluttered with dry bones of humanoids and animals. A band of **30 kobolds** has occupied this old ruin, hiding their plunder (110 cp, 133 sp, 117 gp and a smoky quartz worth 1 gp) here in one of the upper levels. One of the circular sections of the old manor appears to be a large auditorium – one wall is composed of glass bricks. The kobolds inhabit this room, their sleeping furs and cooking fires marring the white marble floors. Another section holds a feast hall and kitchen, the kitchen now occupied by a nest of **three giant vipers**. The third section holds living chambers that must have once been plush, but are now filled with rubble and refuse. This section is also haunted by a strange entity that manifests as a **black cloud** that can produce up to 10 smoky tentacles that can fully manifest into the real world. The touch of this creature causes aging. Although it can move about this section, it cannot leave it. The corpses of a dead wizard and his apprentices can be found here. All are in tattered black robes and turbans. The body of the wizard holds 832 sp, 1,551 gp, 282 pp and a terracotta idol worth 180 gp.

Kobold (30): HD 1d4 hp; AC 6 [13]; **Atk** weapon (1d6); **Move** 6; **Save** 18; **AL** C; **CL/XP** A/5; **Special:** none.

Giant Viper (3): HD 4; AC 5 [14]; **Atk** bite (1d3 + poison); **Move** 12; **Save** 13; **AL** N; **CL/XP** 6/400; **Special:** lethal poison.

Cloud Entity: HD 10; HP 50; AC 0 [19]; **Atk** 10 tentacles (1d4); **Move** 0 (fly 18); **Save** 5; **AL** N; **CL/XP** 14/2600; **Special:** magic resistance (25%), +1 or better weapon to hit.

2018 Guksu

Guksu is the southern spirit of healing, who dwells in a simple hut of stacked, white stones in a pleasant valley of tall grass and wide mesquites. There is a pool here of clear water filled with silver fish. The animal that inhabit the valley have golden fur or scales, and they are quite intelligent. Harming one of them draws the wrath of Guksu, who can prevent one from healing naturally or magically for up to one month. Guksu appears as an old man with a long, red, pointed nose. He appears naked, his body striped with black, white and red paint, and he can take the form of a giant mosquito or a swarm of mosquitos if he wishes. Guksu carries a wand with a tuft of red feathers that also serves as a whistle. With this whistle, he can summon one of the other spirits – Calnis **[32.08]**, Suupadex **[21.02]** or Xa-matutsi **[01.15]** – once per month and request a favor from them. Guksu is a kindly spirit, for the most part, though he dislikes mindless chatter and demands repayment for his services.

Guksu: HD 10; HP 56; AC –2 [21]; **Atk** strike (3d6); **Move** 18 (fly 36); **Save** 5; **AL** N; **CL/XP** 18/3500; **Special:** magic resistance (30%), magical abilities (at will—*detect evil, light*; 3/day—*cure light wounds, mirror image*; 1/day—*charm monster, dispel magic, hold monster, invisibility* (self), *polymorph self, remove curse*), +1 or better weapon to hit.

2102 Suupadax

The northern mountain range hides a strange valley cloaked year-around in ice. The walls of the valley are extremely treacherous, and most folk who attempt to win the valley wind up decorating it with their bones. The valley is the home of the northern whirlwind spirit **Suupadax**, who takes the form of a giant whirlwind with a great, black eye suspended in the middle of it. Suupadax actually dwells in a small, stone lodge in the valley. As one walks towards the lodge, it gets colder and colder, and fires almost always flicker and die. Stepping into the lodge actually sends a person to a demi-dimension of frigid air (or the Elemental Plane of Air, if you prefer). Herein dwells Suupadax, the center of this little cosmos, surrounded by wicked air creatures (sylphs who are a bit ruder than normal sylphs, and who dress like flappers and smoke and consort with mihstu and belkers).

Suupadax is sometimes invoked by wicked spell casters of the region, who come to the periphery of the valley and throw bound, sacrificial victims down the slopes, each having swallowed a gemstone of at least moderate value. They ask the wicked spirit for counsel in treachery and to curse their enemies.

Suupadax: HD 16; HP 78; AC 2 [17]; **Atk** strike (3d8); **Move** 0 (fly 36); **Save** 3; **AL** C; **CL/XP** 19/4100; **Special:** magic resistance (10%), +1 or better weapon to hit, whirlwind.

2109 Diamond House

The "diamond house" is a glass dome that is faceted like a gemstone. The natives call it the diamond house. It stands next to dry river bed filled with small trees and shrubs. From the outside, it looks to hold a pile of gemstones. This is an optical illusion (not magical). During the daytime, the only thing is contains are a number of nearly invisible rays of searing light (save each round or struck for 2d6 points of damage). At night, the interior is safe, but holds nothing of interest. If, however, a powerful magical light is carried within the dome, it emits a single ray of white light that strikes the nearby hills in **[21.07]** and opens a portal in the side of that mountain. This portal leads to the spawning pits of the grimlocks.

2213 Ruined Town

The remnants of a town sit placid beneath the searing sun. One can find many building foundations, but there is little else to see aside from ground glass, bits of metal and stone and a single building that survives as a burned out shell. The Halayans claim that the town was once part of their empire, but was destroyed when the people turned against their faith. The surviving building is the home an old woman named **Mishka**, who happens to be a vampire. She guards several weird stones that look like large geodes. Within these stones are the bodies of **infant vampires**, waiting to be born when their "eggs" are anointed with blood. These infants burst forth as little, feral vampires. There are 15 eggs in all.

Mishka: HD 9; HP 32; AC 2 [17]; **Atk** bite (1d10 + level drain); **Move** 12 (fly 18); **Save** 6; **AL** C; **CL/XP** 12/2000; **Special:** charm gaze, drain 2 levels with hit, gaseous form, only killed in coffin, +1 or better weapon to hit, regenerate (3hp/round), shapeshift, summon rats or wolves.

Infant Vampires: HD 1; **AC** 3 [16]; **Atk** bite (1d4 + sleep); **Move** 6 (fly 9); **Save** 17; **AL** C; **CL/XP** 4/60; **Special:** drain level with hit, gaseous form, only killed in coffin, +1 or silver weapon to hit, regenerate (1hp/round).

2312 Abandoned Velocipede

A velocipede (you know it better as a bicycle) has been abandoned here. Velocipedes are all the rage in Sanctum, having been introduced there a few years back by Mad Morva [38.05]. This one is made of wood and metal, and has a large front wheel and two small back wheels. The wheels are made of wood and reinforced with strips of copper. This particular velocipede needs repairs, and even in working condition would be of little use over the sandy ground of the desert.

2316 Worm Tunnels

The walls of this pass have been bored through by purple worms that clearly turned back upon reaching the dry, hot air of the wastes. In some places, the walls of the pass have collapsed and created small rockslides. A small band of goblin-men is wandering through these tunnels, collecting worm droppings (which can serve as a very long-lasting fuel for fires) using a hand-drawn cart. There is a 2 in 6 chance per hour of running into the **1d6+4 goblin-men** and their cart of worm poop, and a 1 in 20 chance per hour of running into a **purple worm**.

Goblin-Man: HD 1; **AC** 4 [15]; **Atk** weapon (1d6+1); **Move** 12; **Save** 17; **AL** C; **CL/XP** 1/15; **Special:** none.

Purple Worm: HD 15; **HP** 73; **AC** 6 [13]; **Atk** bite (2d12), 1 sting (1d8 + poison); **Move** 9; **Save** 3; **AL** N; **CL/XP** 17/3500; **Special:** poison sting, swallow whole.

2320 False Gods

A number of black, stone idols rise from a patch of creosote and Joshua trees. The idols have been down by wind (and a bit of rain) and are only vaguely humanoid now. All of them are tall and lean, and have hands outstretched and cupped. A small offering left in these hands incurs an old god's wrath, with the sacrificing character suffering a –1 penalty to attacks and saves for 24 hours. If the sacrifice is worth at least 100 gp, the person enjoys a +2 bonus to attacks and saves for 24 hours, followed by a curse (as above) that strikes at each full moon if they do not make an additional sacrifice.

2402 Rock Slide

A rock slide here (perhaps the adventurers will see the great plume of dust when they first enter the hex) has buried the entrance to a dungeon. A large band of dwarf adventurers was buried, though a few managed to escape. Most of the dwarves are normal members of their race, but the key adventurers were fighters and fighter/thieves ranging in level from 2nd to 5th. The dungeon entrance was a small cave. The 30-ft. long tunnel beyond the dungeon entrance opens into a 10-ft. cube room with smoothed walls of sandstone and three revolving doors of solid bronze [A].

[A] This passage is rough hewn. At the intersection there is a small pit holding the burnt remains of the lich Yazzabar. Any fire brought into this passage animates as a small **fire elemental** until the burnt remains are doused with holy water. This can be difficult, for in the presence of fire the charred corpse rises and attacks as a **wight**. The wight has a golden key around his neck.

Fire Elemental: HD 2; **HP** 10; **AC** 2 [17]; **Atk** strike (2d6); **Move** 12; **Save** 16; **AL** N; **CL/XP** 3/60; **Special:** ignite materials.

Wight: HD 3; **HP** 16; **AC** 5 [14]; **Atk** claw (1hp + level drain); **Move** 9; **Save** 14; **AL** C; **CL/XP** 5/240; **Special:** drain 1 level with hit, hit only by magic or silver weapons.

[B] This chamber contains a library of wax tablets, all very fragile.

In all, there are 100 such tablets, some containing mystic secrets and formulae, some containing histories of the region, and others containing chants that seem to make no sense. The room also contains a deep well of black energy. Anyone in the room is attacked by the **tendrils of energy** (they attack as a 3 HD monster), and if struck must pass a saving throw or have a portion of the life and personality stolen away and inscribed on a blank tablet as one of those nonsensical chants. In essence, this counts as level drain. To regain these levels, one must search through the tablets (cumulative 1% chance per round per person searching) to find the one holding their essence and read it. Reading a different person's tablet does not bestow their life energy upon you. If a wax tablet is destroyed, that portion of the person's soul is also destroyed. The tendrils can be held back by a cleric using his or her turn undead ability (treat as a 6 HD undead) or a tendril can be stunned for 1d4 rounds with a splash of holy water or for 1d8 rounds with a holy weapon.

[C] This room contains a twelve glass spheres. Each one contains an insect (**spider**, **centipede**, **scorpion** or **wasp**) and a tiny chest. Touching a sphere transports a person into the sphere where they must fight the "giant insect". Grabbing a chest after a battle transports a person back outside the sphere (at normal size). The chests can be opened by the key found in [A], and contain 1d4 x 100 gp each.

Man-sized Giant Centipede (7ft): HD 2; **HP** 8; **AC** 5[14]; **Atk** bite (1d8 + poison); **Move** 15; **Save** 16; **AL** N; **CL/XP** 4/120; **Special:** poison bite (+6 save or die).

Giant Scorpion: HD 6; **HP** 40; **AC** 3[16]; **Atk** 2 pincers (1d10), sting (1d4 + poison); **Move** 12; **Save** 11; **AL** N; **CL/XP** 8/800; **Special:** lethal poison sting.

Giant Spider (4ft diameter): HD 2+2; **HP** 10; **AC** 6[13]; **Atk** bite (1d6 + poison); **Move** 18; **Save** 16; **AL** N; **CL/XP** 5/240; **Special:** lethal poison, 5 in 6 chance to surprise prey.

Giant Wasp: HD 4; **HP** 20; **AC** 4[15]; **Atk** sting (1d4 + poison), bite (1d8); **Move** 1 (fly 20); **Save** 13; **AL** N; **CL/XP** 6/400; **Special:** paralyzing poison, larvae.

[D] This room's only contents are two statues; one represents a scholarly man, the other a stern, though attractive, woman. The man was Yazzabar, who became a lich. The woman was Amphiba, a zealous cleric of Law, who was once his lover. Passing between the statues (they flank the western door) causes a person to be struck by pink lightning emitted from their eyes. This deals 2d6 points of damage, and forces a male to save or have the memories and personality of chaotic Yazzabar implanted into them, or if female the memories and personality of lawful Amphiba implanted in them. This does not give them magic-user or cleric powers, and can be countered by a *remove curse* spell or *wish*.

[E] Five people, probably magic-users from the look of them, are suspended here from the ceiling. They have been dipped in wax along with their spellbooks. Each of them was a rival of Yazzabar. Assume their spellbooks contain a daily complement of spells for a magic-user of 1d4+1 level. The books must be released from the wax to be used, and doing so has a 1 in 6 chance of infecting a person with mummy rot. Magic is suppressed in this room, which is guarded by a **clockwork gorilla**.

Clockwork Gorilla: HD 8; **HP** 36; **AC** 1 [18]; **Atk** 2 hands (1d6) and bite (2d6); **Move** 12; **Save** 8; **AL** N; **CL/XP** 8/800; **Special:** hug and rend, immune to mind effects, poison and disease.

2406 Ruined Fortress

The mountain pass here is guarded by a fortress that spans the pass. The fortress is about 200 feet wide and 100 feet tall, with a lower span of battlements about 50 feet above the ground. The castle is composed of the native rock, and was built expertly, possibly by dwarves. In the middle of the fortress, on either side, there is a massive set of doors (thick oak, bound in spiked steel), and between them a 40 ft. long court. Iron doors (locked) on either side of the courtyard grant access into the fortress. The

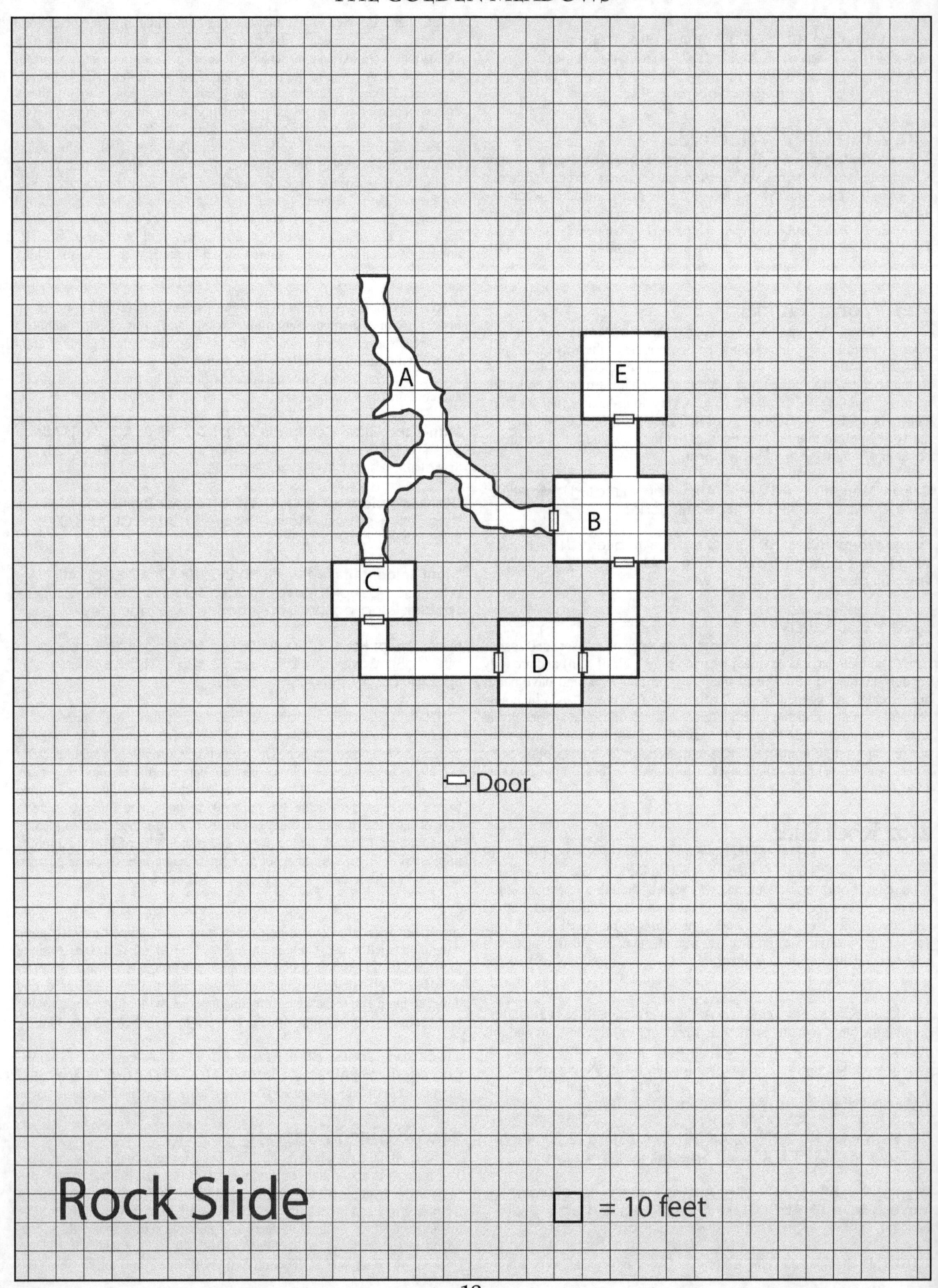

Rock Slide

☐ = 10 feet

place carries the smell of death, and indeed is filled with the skeletal remains of about 300 dwarf warriors, most still in their ring mail or chainmail armor, hand axes, warhammers, short swords and other weapons still in their grasp. Each of them has a pentagram carved or drawn onto their foreheads, and similar graffiti can be found throughout the place. It is now used by a chaos cult from Sanctum, who, once every year at the summer solstice, travel to the fortress to sacrifice a maiden to a **chuul** who dwells in a pit here. The chuul was summoned from nether dimensions and is bound in its pit, unable to escape, though the cult leader **Vermes**, a charismatic merchant is working on breaking this binding. Various **chaos beasts** roam the halls of the fortress, ready to give battle to intruders (they leave the cultists alone). The cultists normally number **three 2nd level clerics, six 1st level clerics and twelve normal humans**, all of them in crimson robes with pointed hoods and wearing leather armor under their robes.

Vermes (Clr6): HP 24; AC 4 [15]; **Atk** warhammer (1d4+2); **Save** 10; **AL** C; **CL/XP** 7/600; **Special:** banish undead, +2 vs. paralysis and poison, spells (2/2/1/1).
> **Spells:** 1st—*cure light wounds, protection from good;* 2nd—*hold person x2;* 3rd—*prayer;* 4th—*cure serious wounds.*
> **Equipment:** chain mail, shield, *+1 warhammer.*

Cultist cleric (Clr2) (3): HP 10; AC 7 [12]; **Atk** heavy mace (1d4+1) or throwing hammer (1d4); **Save** 14; **AL** C; **CL/XP** 2/30; **Special:** banish undead, +2 vs. paralysis and poison, spells (1).
> **Spells:** 1st—*charm person.*
> **Equipment:** leather armor, shield, heavy mace, 3 throwing hammers, unholy symbol.

Cultist cleric (Clr1) (6): HP 5; AC 7 [12]; **Atk** light mace (1d4); **Save** 15; **AL** C; **CL/XP** 7/600; **Special:** banish undead, +2 vs. paralysis and poison.
> **Equipment:** Leather armor, light mace, unholy symbol.

Cultists: HD 1; AC 7 [12]; **Atk** short sword (1d6) or dagger (1d4); **Save** 17; **AL** C; **CL/XP** 1/15; **Special:** none.
> **Equipment:** leather armor, short sword, dagger, unholy symbol.

Chuul: HD 10; hp 76; AC 2[17]; **Atk** 2 pincers (1d6), bite (1d8), paralytic tentacles; **Move** 15 (swim 12); **Save** 5; **AL** N; **CL/XP** 11/1700; **Special:** Immune to poison; tentacle grab.

Chaos Beast: HD 16; HP 92; AC –2 [21]; **Atk** 4 claws (1d8 + corporeal instability); **Move** 9; **Save** 3; **AL** N; **CL/XP** 21/4700; **Special:** amorphous (immune to backstabs), corporeal instability (save or become spongy, amorphous mass and lose 1 point of wisdom per round; save each round to regain normalcy; at 0 wisdom, effect is permanent), immune to polymorph and petrification, magic resistance (45%).

2510 Spirit House

A coven of druids has built a sweat lodge here. Each of the druids represents one of the peoples of the region; there is a Vegan female called **Da'szabor**, a goblin-man male called **Thurk** (an outcast from his people) and the human druid **Corvin** from Sanctum (a short man with blazing red hair and friendly, though mildly crazy eyes). The druids are in communing with the four great spirits of the region, Guksu, Calnis, Suupadax and Xa-matutsi, attempting to learn from them the mystic dances they must perform, and the times of those performances, to keep them friendly.

Da'szabor, Vegan Female (Drd6): HP 17; AC 6 [13]; **Atk** spear (1d6) or sling (1d4); **Save** 10; **AL** N; **CL/XP** 6/400; **Special:** 1/day—*ESP,* first mysteries, immune to fey charms, +2 vs. fire, shapechange, spells (3/2/2).
> **Spells:** 1st—*faerie fire x2, locate animals;* 2nd—*cure light wounds, heat metal;* 3rd—*call lightning x2.*
> **Equipment:** leather armor, shield, spear, sling, holy

symbol.

Thurk, Goblin-Man (Drd4): HP 14; AC 6 [13]; **Atk** spear (1d6) or sling (1d4); **Save** 12; **AL** N; **CL/XP** 4/120; **Special:** first mysteries, spells (3/1/1).
> **Spells:** 1st—*detect magic, faerie fire, predict weather;* 2nd—*speak with animals;* 3rd—*hold animal.*
> **Equipment:** Leather armor, shield, short sword, sling, holy symbol.

Corvin (Drd8): HP 28; AC 3 [16]; **Atk** spear (1d6) or sling (1d4); **Save** 8; **AL** N; **CL/XP** 9/1100; **Special:** first mysteries, immune to fey charms, +2 vs. fire, shapechange, spells (4/3/2/1).
> **Spells:** 1st—*faerie fire x2, locate animals x2;* 2nd—*cure light wounds, heat metal x2;* 3rd—*call lightning, plant growth;* 4th—*plant doorway.*
> **Equipment:** Leather armor, shield, short sword, sling, holy symbol.

2619 White Caves

These chalk caves capture the shadows of creatures that enter and spend more than 10 minutes within, assuming they have a light source with which to cast those shadows. The **shadows** never leave the cave, but rather creep back into a deep cavern where they serve as the guardians of a well of black water. The water roils when people approach it. It can heal all wounds and negative effects, but a character must be lowered into the water and suspended for 3 days, during which time they seem to expire. When removed at the end of three days, they are restored to life and perfect health. During this time, the person is assaulted by terrible nightmares, and must pass one saving throw per day or permanently lose 1 point of wisdom.

Shadow: HD 3+3; AC 7 [12]; **Atk** touch (1d4 + strength drain); **Move** 12; **Save** 14; **AL** C; **CL/XP** 4/120; **Special:** drain 1 point str with hit, +1 or better weapon to hit.

2712 Killer Shrimp

The skeleton of a giant catfish is bobbing on the surface here, having been picked clean by a swarm of **killer shrimp**. A net has become tangled with the skeleton. It contains several glass spheres, one of them a crystal ball. The swarm fills a 20-ft. diameter hemisphere (or 10-ft. diameter sphere if completely submerged) and swarms on any living creature it can reach.

Killer Shrimp Swarm: HD 4; AC 2 [17]; **Atk** swarm (1d8); **Move** 0 (swim 9); **Save** 13; **AL** N; **CL/XP** 5/240; **Special:** no damage from slashing and piercing weapons, minimum damage from bludgeoning weapons.

2722 Grimlock Caves

A long shaft leads into an ancient network of mines that are now inhabited by a tribe of **50 grimlocks** and their cabal of **three mind eater masters**. The mind eaters dwell on the lower levels of the mine complex, that once produced gold and silver, but which is now empty. There is a large slave population here and three slave pits. The grimlocks and their slaves are slowly constructing a crystalline matrix that fills a long, round tunnel. As one walks through the tunnel, their vision becomes wavy and a wave of nausea sweeps over them, as they feel space being twisted out of shape. The tunnel, when complete and fully powered, will act as a time tunnel, permitting the mind eaters to travel forward or backward to acquire either weird technologies from the future or powerful artifacts from the past. The tunnel is about 50% complete. The grimlocks require gemstones of rare quality to complete their matrix. A captive **time elemental**, held within an iron flask until it is needed and properly sequestered in the matrix, will power the device.

Grimlock: HD 2; AC 7 [12]; **Atk** weapon (1d8); **Move** 12; **Save** 16; **AL** C; **CL/XP** 2/30; **Special:** can sense creatures and objects within 40 ft., immune to gaze attacks.

Mind Eater: HD 8; **HP** 40, 35, 34; **AC** 5 [14]; **Atk** 4 tentacles (2hp); **Move** 12; **Save** 8; **AL** C; **CL/XP** 12/2000; **Special:** eat brains, magic resistance (90%), mental blast, mental powers.

Time Elemental: HD 12; **HP** 63; **AC** 0 [19]; **Atk** 2 slams (2d6 + cell death); **Move** 0 (fly 9); **Save** 3; **AL** N; **CL/XP** 20/4400; **Special:** cell death, foresight, immunity to magic, magic resistance (40%), multimanifestation, +1 or better weapon to hit, time jaunt.

2801 Stone Bones

The petrified **skeleton** of an ichthyosaur lurks beneath the sands here. Animated long ago by a necromancer, it guards the hex from intruders, for hidden deeper beneath the sands there is a large bunker complex that the necromancer used as his base of operations. The bunker can be reached most easily by teleportation, but if one could clear the sands to a depth of 10 feet, they might find an iron trapdoor. The bunker is inhabited by a few dozen skeletal guards, as well as other, more dangerous undead, who guard a small treasure and armory (five pikes, seven suits of splinted chainmail, 10,000 cp, 2,000 sp, 180 gp, a small clock and a small agate worth 40 gp), a library containing a couple old spellbooks (each holds 16 levels worth of spells, from level 1 to 4) and a laboratory.

Ichthyosaur Skeleton: HD 12; **HP** 51; **AC** 6 [13]; **Atk** bite (3d6); **Move** 9 (burrow 24); **Save** 3; **AL** N; **CL/XP** 12/2000; **Special:** none.

2808 Bubbling Idol

There is a sinkhole here, at the bottom of which is a foaming pool of brackish water. The source of the foaming appears to be a strange, abstract idol that looks something like solidified green flame. The surface of the idol bubbles and pops, and green slime flows from it into the pond. **Five walking slimes**, the priests of their people (they cast spells as 5th level druids), can be found here much of the time, communing with their slimy deity. Caves branch from here into the suburbs of Slime City, which is located further below the ground and is said to be ruled by the most ancient of black puddings, a lake-sized entity whose wishes are interpreted by a legion of priests.

Walking Slime Priests (5): HD 5; **HP** 22, 17, 19, 13, 15; **AC** 9 [11]; **Atk** touch (1d6 + turn to slime); **Move** 6; **Save** 12; **AL** N; **CL/XP** 8/800; **Special:** cast spells as 5th level druid (3/2/1), transform to slime.

    Spells: 1st—*faerie fire x3*; 2nd—*heat metal, produce flame*; 3rd—*protection against fire*.

2904 Ghost Town

An old mining town has been abandoned here. The town consists of about 30 stone huts gathered around a mine shaft. The mine shaft descends about 60 feet into the ground (via a pulley system that is quite worn and very unsafe). At the bottom of the shaft, there are three exploratory tunnels, one of which shows signs of a meager vein of silver (a dwarf can determine this easily). This tunnel has caved in. The miners lost in the cave-in still dwell in these tunnels as **three specters**. If driven away, the mine could be reopened, and would produce about 1d10 x 5 gp worth of silver (after refinement) per month if worked by at least six humans (or three dwarves).

Spectre: HD 7; **HP** 25, 34, 33; **AC** 2[17]; **Atk** spectral weapon or touch (1d8 + level drain); **Move** 15 (fly 30); **Save** 9; **AL** C; **CL/XP** 9/1100; **Special:** drain 2 levels with hit, +1 or better weapon to hit.

3009 Orchard of Blood

A valley here in the deep mountains is well watered by springs and filled with willow-like trees with coppery bark and dark green leaves. The branches are heavy with bunches of berries that look like white grapes. These berries are red on the inside and their flesh tastes of blood. Strange,

gaunt **squirrels** inhabit these trees and favor these berries. When they are stolen, these creatures become quite irate and attack the invaders, revealing that they are also fond of humanoid blood. The only other inhabitants of the valley are a band of haggard-looking vampires. The vampires were once human adventurers who sampled the berries – each berry that is eaten carries with it a 5% chance of infecting the eater with a blood disease that slowly transforms them into vampires over the course of 30 days. There are **12 vampires** in all, who come out at night to feed on the berries while the squirrels slumber. Their cave holds a treasure of 1,940 sp, 150 gp and a platinum ewer worth 950 gp as well as a roll of papers revealing the identities of the chaos cultists of Sanctum.

Squirrels: HD 1d4; **AC** 7 [12]; **Atk** bite (1d3 + blood drain); **Move** 12; **Save** 18; **AL** N; **CL/XP** A/5; **Special:** blood drain (1d3 points of damage per round).

Vampires (12): HD 7; **AC** 2 [17]; **Atk** bite (1d10 + level drain); **Move** 12 (fly 18); **Save** 9; **AL** C; **CL/XP** 10/1400; **Special:** charm gaze, drain 2 levels with hit, gaseous form, only killed in coffin, +1 or better weapon to hit, regenerate (3hp/ round), shapeshift, summon rats or wolves.

3012 Submerged Cave

A partially submerged cave here on the shore holds a multitude of cave carvings that present a map to the catacombs in the center of the Golden Meadow. The cave is inhabited by a **giant catfish** which the locathah have nicknamed Lucifer. Lucifer has a few skeletons in his cave, and one of them carries a rusted iron flask that hides a small sapphire worth 200 gp.

Giant Catfish: HD 7; **HP** 44; **AC** 6 [13]; **Atk** bite (1d10) and shock (1d6); **Move** 0 (swim 12); **Save** 11; **AL** N; **CL/XP** 8/800; **Special:** can generate a shock once per 3 rounds.

3018 Coruscating Falls

A small waterfall is located here. The water is multi-colored and spills into a shallow pool. The pool is covered by an oily sheen that is actually a **sentient entity**. It is terribly wise and can communicate telepathically. The creature could be destroyed with fire, but it is not dangerous.

3021 Amazon Camp

A **war party** of red amazons has made camp here. They have traveled from the wastelands to the southeast and seek loot and glory. The group is commanded by **Azrash** and her sister-wife, **Horeth**. They command **ten amazon warriors**, and all are mounted on light warhorses.

Azrash, Female (Ftr7): HP 32; **AC** 4 [15]; **Atk** 2 spear attacks (1d8) or short bow x2 (1d6); **Save** 8; **AL** C; **CL/XP** 7/600, **Special:** multiple attacks, parry.
> **Equipment:** chain mail, shield, spear, short bow, 10 arrows.

Horeth, Female (Clr6): HP 20; **AC** 4 [15]; **Atk** warhammer (1d4+1); **Save** 10; **AL** C; **CL/XP** 7/600; **Special:** banish undead, +2 vs. paralysis and poison, spells (2/2/1/1).
> **Spells:** 1st—*cure light wounds* x2; 2nd—*hold person* x2; 3rd—*cure disease, remove curse*; 4th—*neutralize poison*.
> **Equipment:** chain mail, shield, warhammer.

Red Amazons (10): HD 1+1; **AC** 2 [17]; **Atk** 2 spear attacks (1d8) or short bow x2 (1d6); **Move** 12; **Save** 17; **AL** C; **CL/XP** 1/15; **Special:** none.

War Horse: HD 3; **AC** 7 [12]; **Atk** bite (1d2), 2 hooves (1d3); **Move** 18; **Save** 15; **AL** N; **CL/XP** 3/60; **Special:** none.

3116 Gold Mine

A band of grimlocks is working a deep gold mine here, using human beings as their beasts of burden. The grimlocks have a fortified cavern underground, with various mining tunnels and shafts radiating out from it, and a series of slave pits located beneath it in a sort of dungeon arrangements. Most of the human laborers have had their minds scrambled by the mind eaters, and are thus virtual zombies. A few still have their minds, but are careful to hide this fact. In all, there are **40 grimlocks** armed with picks, and 50 humans used as pack animals. One is called **Yasbin**. She was drugged in a tavern in Sanctum and woke up here. Her thief skills saved her from a visit by the mind eaters, but she is still shackled and without her tools. There is also a human merchant named **Zixby** (a rival of Vermes) and a silversmith of the golden men of the south called **Oomphalz**. The grimlocks acquire their slaves from unscrupulous traders of Sanctum (among them Vermes), who trade slaves for gold. The entrance to the mine has a *phantasmal force* cast over it that resembles a green demonic face with an open mouth. The mouth is pitch black (even to darkvision) and seems to radiate intense cold. All of this is an illusion to keep snoopers out of the mine. Eight grimlock warriors wait within the entrance. They are armed with stone axes and a net, and will try first to waylay and enslave explorers.

Grimlocks (40): HD 2; **AC** 7 [12]; **Atk** weapon (1d8); **Move** 12; **Save** 16; **AL** C; **CL/XP** 2/30; **Special:** can sense creatures and objects within 40 ft, immune to gaze attacks.

Yasbin (Thf4): HP 3 (9 normally); **AC** 9 [10]; **Atk** fist (1); **Save** 12; **AL** N; **CL/XP** 4/120; **Special:** backstab (x2), +2 save vs. traps, thieving abilities.
> **Thieving Abilities:** Climb 88%, Tasks 30%, Hear 4 in 6, Hide 25%, Silent 35%, Locks 25%.
> **Equipment:** none

Zixby: HD 3; **HP** 10; **AC** 9 [10]; **Atk** fist (1); **Move** 12; **Save** 14; **AL** N; **CL/XP** 3/60; **Special:** none.

Oomphalz, Golden Man: HD 1d4hp; **HP** 3; **AC** 9 [10]; **Atk** weapon (1d4); **Save** 18; **AL** N; **CL/XP** B/10; **Special:** none.

3202 Halayan Camp

A band of Halayan trappers has made camp here on their way to Sanctum, where they plan to live it up for a couple days away from their saintly wives. They number **12 hunters**, armed with their long muskets and hand axes, and are carrying about 200 gp worth of pelts and skins to trade, along with sacks containing 120 silver coins, not to mention bedrolls and blankets, about 3 days of iron rations, tinder boxes, flint and steel, etc. Unlike the traders, they wear only leather armor.

Halayan Hunter (12): HD 2; **AC** 7 [12]; **Atk** musket (1d10) or hand axe (1d6); **Move** 15; **Save** 16; **AL** N; **CL/XP** 2/30; **Special:** surprise on 1–2 on 1d6, surprised on 1 on 1d10, track as 6th level ranger.

3208 Calnis

Calnis is the eastern spirit of mischief, who appears either as a handsome man in a cloak of crow feathers or as a black feathered serpent. Calnis dwells in the eastern mountains in a temple of black stone with a silver portal. The temple is guarded by black-feathered **harpies**, who demand offerings of fresh meat and pretty things. Once inside the building, petitioners discover that it is much larger than they could have imagined, a great hall of black marble and silver trimmings. There is no roof here, just a night sky illuminated by a full moon that seems to close you could reach out and touch it. The room swirls with dancing spirits (treat them as **spectres** if adventurers are stupid enough to attack). A black throne in the center of the great hall is the perch of Calnis, usually in human form, who beckons the petitioners forward that he might mock their pitiful pleas. Those who meet his gaze must pass a save or begin dancing uncontrollably, losing 1 hit point per round until they have but one hit point left, and then losing 1 point of constitution per round until they die at 0 constitution. To receive a favor from Calnis, one must tell him a good riddle, or in some other way trick him. They must also accept a curse in return for his favor.

Calnis: HD 10; **HP** 58; **AC** 0 [19]; **Atk** bite (2d6 + poison), tail (1d6 constrict); **Move** 12 (fly 24); **Save** 8; **AL** N; **CL/XP** 14/2600; **Special:** fly, magical abilities (1/day—*charm person, ESP, invisibility, shield, sleep, suggestion*), poison, polymorph.

Harpy: HD 3; **AC** 7[12]; **Atk** 2 talons (1d3) and weapon (1d6); **Move** 6 (fly 18); **Save** 14; **AL** C; **CL/XP** 4/120; **Special:** flight, siren-song.

Spectre: HD 7; **AC** 2[17]; **Atk** spectral weapon or touch (1d8 + level drain); **Move** 15 (fly 30); **Save** 9; **AL** C; **CL/XP** 9/1100; **Special:** drain 2 levels with hit, +1 or better weapon to hit.

3305 Valley of Fire

The valley of fire is a wide valley of sandstone walls and sandstone rock formations, all of them red-orange in color, and some resembling fantastic beasts or fairy castles. This alone could give the valley its name, but it is also filled with a flaming gas to a depth of about 5 feet. The gas flows from below the ground, and though the upper portions flow red and orange, the lower portions are blue and extremely hot. Falling into the fire means certain death to any who are not immune to fire. One of the larger rock formations in the valley is used as a small tower by a band of **azer** who use the roiling blue flames to work adamantine and mithral.

Azer: HD 2; **AC** 1 [18]; **Atk** heavy mace (1d8) or fists (1d4); **Move** 12; **Save** 16; **AL** N; **CL/XP** 3/60; **Special:** double damage from cold attacks, immune to fire, magic resistance (5%).

3320 Quartz Forest

The ground in this hex begins to descend as it nears the highlands, eventually funneling into a vast system of caves. Most of the caves are narrow, with low ceilings, but a few are more easily traversed and lead to a large cavern about 200 feet below the surface. The cavern is quite cold and completely dry. About one hundred quartz pillars run from floor to ceiling. A dwarf can tell that the cavern was carved by some agent, maybe as much as 500 years ago. Some of the pillars are trapped to collapse if leaned upon or chipped at (1 in 6 chance; collapsing pillar does 6d6 damage, save for half). One of the pillars has been enchanted. If touched, all creatures within 30 feet suffer a delusion. They see the most fearsome thing they can imagine charging at them. If they run (player's choice), their fear will carry them out of the cavern and into the maze of tunnels, where there is a percentage chance equal to 35 minus their wisdom score that they become hopelessly lost. If they stand fast, the creature washes over them as a weird energy, leaving them hairless (permanently) and with a strange blue mark on their heads – something like a crescent moon. The mind eaters and grimlocks will recognize this sign and regard those who bear it as worthies to be respected and, of course, devoured after the proper ceremonies have been carried out. The marked characters will also enjoy a +2 bonus to save vs. psionic-type effects.

3413 Smuggler's Cove

A band of **smugglers** operates from this cove. They have about 500 gp worth of contraband here (pelts, grain, glassware), as well as an locked iron chest (trapped with a poison needle) containing 300 sp and 75 gp. The smugglers are led by Bonny Beph, who is currently in the custody of the bounty hunter Mazbury **[37.14]**. The smugglers are in a bad mood, and Beph's lieutenants, **Yolf** and **Krand**, are on the brink of fighting for control of the gang. The smugglers would rather have Beph back.

Smugglers, Males or Females (12): HD 1d4; AC 7 [12]; Atk short sword (1d6) or shortbow x2 (1d6); **Move** 12; **Save** 18; **AL** N; **CL/XP** B/10; **Special:** surprise on 1–3 on 1d6.
> **Equipment:** leather armor, short sword, shortbow, 10 arrows, thieves' tools.

Yolf (Thf3): HP 9; AC 7 [12]; **Atk** short sword (1d6) or dagger (1d4) or dart (1d3); **Save** 13; **AL** C; **CL/XP** 2/30; **Special:** backstab (x2), +2 save vs. traps, read languages, thieving abilities.
> **Thieving Abilities:** Climb 87%, Tasks 25%, Hear 4 in 6, Hide 20%, Silent 30%, Locks 20%.
> **Equipment:** leather armor, short sword, 3 daggers, 5 darts, thieves' tools.

Krand (Thf4): HP 8; AC 7 [12]; **Atk** short sword (1d6) or dagger (1d4); **Save** 12; **AL** N; **CL/XP** 3/60; **Special:** backstab (x2), +2 save vs. traps, read languages, thieving abilities.
> **Thieving Abilities:** Climb 88%, Tasks 30%, Hear 4 in 6, Hide 25%, Silent 35%, Locks 25%.
> **Equipment:** leather armor, short sword, 2 daggers, thieves' tools.

3501 Brothel

Adventurers may come across a circle of stone longhouses. The longhouses are a brothel, where the wizard **Malphas** has trained a wondrous menagerie of creatures in tantric secrets that, when practiced, thin the barriers between this world and another. The menagerie includes a haughty salamander called **Yizbard**, twin mermaids called **Ophelia** and **Lily** (their longhouse contains a pool), a highborn **Venusian lady** (green skin, four arms), a fallen deva named **Uzrakiel** (he has lost his wings), a sylph named **Ephemera** held in her house by a silver chain, two handsome men named **Uth'laktru** and **Pekhmar** covered with spines and man with silver skin and black eyes called **Novom**. The prices here are quite affordable, and the services are only occasionally lethal. Each time a service is used, there is a 1% chance that the hex will be filled with stinging, purple mists that will slowly (over the course of 24 hours) manifest as a gargantuan lamia noble called **Bavylos**, the goddess of a demi-plane of lust who will endeavor to make a new home for herself in this plane.

Malphas (MU7): HP 20; AC 9 [10]; **Atk** staff (1d6) or dagger (1d4) or dart (1d3); **Save** 9; **AL** C; **CL/XP** 7/600; **Special:** +2 vs. spells, spells (4/3/2/1).
> **Spells:** 1st—*charm person, light, magic missile x2*; 2nd—*detect invisibility, mirror image x2*; 3rd—*dispel magic, hold person*; 4th—*charm monster*
> **Equipment:** staff, silver dagger, 2 daggers, 6 darts, spellbook.

Yizbard, Salamander Female: HD 7; HP 38; AC 5 [14] (torso); 3 [16] (serpent body); **Atk** touch and constrict (2d8 + 1d6 heat) or weapon (1d6); **Move** 9; **Save** 9; **AL** C; **CL/XP** 8/800; **Special:** heat, constrict.

Ophelia and Lily, Mermaid Females: HD 1+3; HP 9, 8; AC 7 [12]; **Atk** dagger (1d4); **Move** 1 (swim 18); **Save** 17; **AL** N; **CL/XP** 1/15; **Special:** breathe water.
> **Equipment:** dagger

Venusian Lady, Venusian Female: HD 1; HP 4; AC 9 [10]; **Atk** 2 slams (1d3); **Move** 12; **Save** 17; **AL** N; **CL/XP** 1/15; **Special:** speak with plants.

Uzrakiel, Deva Male: HD 12; HP 57; AC –3 [22]; **Atk** slam (1d10); **Move** 21 (no flight); **Save** 3; **AL** N; **CL/XP** 13/2300; **Special:** cannot fly due to missing wings, immune to acid, cold and paralysis.

Ephemera, Sylph Female: HD 3; HP 19; AC 9 [10]; **Atk** fist (1); **Move** 12 (fly 36); **Save** 14; **AL** N; **CL/XP** 5/240; **Special:** conjure 8 HD air elemental 1/day, invisibility 1/day, immune to poison gas.

Uth'laktru and Pekhmar, Man-Urchin Males: HD 2; HP 8; AC 8 [11]; **Atk** slam (1d4); **Move** 12; **Save** 16; **AL** N; **CL/XP** 3/60; **Special:** those in melee combat with them must pass a save each round or suffer 1 point of damage from their spines.

Novum, Mercurial Male: HD 4; HP 20; AC 2 [17]; **Atk** slam (1d4+1); **Move** 12; **Save** 13; **AL** C; **CL/XP** 5/240; **Special:** gaze attack (save or affect by *suggestion*)

Bavylos, lamia noble female goddess: HD 18; HP 84; AC 3 [16]; **Atk** 2 claws (1d12); **Move** 30; **Save** 3; **AL** C; **CL/XP** 21/4700; **Special:** magical abilities (3/day—*charm person, charm monster, suggestion*), touch drains 1d4 wisdom for 1d6 days.

3503 Night Gaunt Canyon

This portion of the Red River runs through a canyon with steep, towering walls. There are narrow beaches on the sides of the canyon, and they are littered with wreckage from barges and keelboats. At night, the canyon is filled with fluttering **nightgaunts**, who snatch at folk moving down the river and carry them wherever the Referee would like them to go. One of the smaller caves in the canyon walls is the entrance to a shrine of Tsathogga, a shrine tended by an old hermit with a lazy eye and fetid breath. The hermit is called **Azbik**, and he serves the chaos cult of Sanctum, who make their way to the spot during the new moon to give offerings of gold and blood to the frog god. An elf might notice blackened iron spikes pounded into the wall beneath the cave.

The cave extends back 20 feet and then opens into a temple of polished stone. There is an altar festooned with black candles atop human skulls. Azbik sleeps on a straw mat in front of the idol. He has a silver flute that summons a **black pudding** up from a deep pit, about 2 feet in diameter, located in the center of the temple.

Azbik (Clr9): HP 22; AC 2 [17]; **Atk** +2 *light mace* (1d4+2); **Save** 7; **AL** C; **CL/XP** 10/1400; **Special:** banish undead, +2 poison and paralyzation, spells (3/3/3/2/2).
> **Spells:** 1st—*cure light wounds x3*; 2nd—*hold person x3*;

3rd—*prayer, speak with the dead x2*; 4th—*cure serious wounds, protection form good, 10 ft radius*; 5th—*finger of death x2.*
Equipment: plate mail, shield, +2 *light mace* (allows Azbik to become a cloud of flies, 1/day – per *gaseous form* spell), unholy symbol.

Nightgaunt: HD 4; **AC** 5 [14]; **Atk** 2 claws (1d4) and tail (1d4 + submission); **Move** 12 (fly 21); **Save** 13; **AL** C; **CL/XP** 6/400; **Special:** magic resistance (5%), submission (save or stunned for 1d4 rounds), surprise on 1–3 on 1d6.

Black Pudding: HD 10; **HP** 48; **AC** 6 [13]; **Atk** attack (3d8); **Move** 6; **Save** 5; **AL** N; **CL/XP** 11/1700; **Special:** acidic surface, divides when hit with lightning, immune to cold.

3606 Locathah

The locathah have a watch station here, near the shore. The locals know about it, and only a novice navigator would ever run into with their boat. The station is a stout tower that rises to within 3 feet of the surface. It is built of cut stone of various textures and colors, giving it a patchwork appearance. Three trident-armed locathah are always to be found atop the tower, occasionally poking their heads above the water to keep an eye on things. The locals usually know them by name (one can tell them apart by their tendrils and skin patterns), and they often stop to talk and trade a little tobacco (the locathah like to chew it) for some fish or simply for their goodwill of the locathah. In total, **twenty locathah** are assigned to the watch tower, one of them being the **commander** (3 HD) and two **sub-commanders** (2 HD). They wear mail ponchos (made of bronze rings) and are armed with tridents and light crossbows.

Locathah (20): HD 1; **AC** 6 [13]; **Atk** trident (1d6) or light crossbow (1d8); **Move** 12 (swim 18); **Save** 17; **AL** N; **CL/XP** 1/15; **Special:** none.
Equipment: bronze mail poncho, trident.

Locathah sub-commanders (2): HD 2; **HP** 8, 11; **AC** 6 [13]; **Atk** trident (1d6) or light crossbow (1d8); **Move** 12 (swim 18); **Save** 16; **AL** N; **CL/XP** 2/30; **Special:** none.
Equipment: bronze mail poncho, trident.

Locathah commander: HD 3; **HP** 17; **AC** 6 [13]; **Atk** +1 *trident* (1d6+1) or light crossbow (1d8); **Move** 12 (swim 18); **Save** 14; **AL** N; **CL/XP** 3/60; **Special:** none.
Equipment: bronze mail poncho, +1 *trident*, coral crown (worth 125 gp).

3611 Golden Man Ship from South

Three keelboats are making their way across the lake. They carry trade goods of the golden men of the south, mostly leather goods (including armor, whips, sandals, boots, etc.) and dried fungus (some edible, some poisonous, some hallucinogenic). The three boats were ported from the Red River over a range of mountains and around the ancient dam that created the lake. Each of the boats has a **captain** and **three crewmen**, all armed. They also carry with them a secret message for the lord mayor of Sanctum from the Emperor of the South.

Crewmen: HD 1; **HP** 4x2, 3; **AC** 6 [13]; **Atk** scimitar (1d8) and curved dagger (1d4); **Move** 12; **Save** 17; **AL** N; **CL/XP** 1/15; **Special:** none.

Captain: HD 5; **HP** 29; **AC** 5 [14]; **Atk** scimitar (1d8) and curved dagger (1d4); **Move** 12; **Save** 12; **AL** N; **CL/XP** 5/240; **Special:** none.

3704 Sanctum

Sanctum is a small, rollicking town (pop. 1,500) on the shores of the lake, where all sorts of folk from the surrounding lands meet to trade.

Large caravans gather here to make the torturous journey into the eastern lands, over the mountains, to trade for exotic goods. The village is composed of about 100 odd buildings constructed of stones, bricks, timber (some of it driftwood) and whatever else the people could find. The town has no enemies, so it has no defensive walls, though it does have about **20 men-at-arms** (some of them ex-buccaneers) who patrol the town. They wear ring armor and carry spears and short bows.

The largest building in the town is a stone counting house, where merchants gather to trade goods and change money as needed. Next to this building stands the manor house (a 3-story Victorian that has seen better days) of **Grubnitz, the Lord Mayor,** a money-grubbing old lout who, nonetheless, has a keen mind and fine organizational skills. The town has cobblestone streets that are traversed by the colorful cattle of the southerners, the century worms of the westerners, pack mules led by prospectors, and the local well-to-do on Mad Marva's latest invention, the velocipede (which you know as bicycles). The streets are usually thick with people visiting the many taverns and gambling houses, traders, mercenaries and craftsmen. The food tends to be salty and the booze is often watered down, but in all the place presents a festive atmosphere, and considering that it is the last post of civilization for many days in any direction.

One can find just about anything they need to buy in Sanctum, though the prices are usually 2 to 5 times normal (roll 1d4+1) due to the transportation costs and the paucity of resources. Sanctum boasts a number of small temples dedicated to a wide variety of deities (Arauc, the god of trade and patron deity of the town, Akatele, the irascible sky god with a heart of gold worshiped by the golden men of the south, the faceless and nameless blood goddess of the golden men of the west, the Great Spirit of the Halayans, and many gods and goddesses who probably had their origin in the drug-addled minds of their prophets), as well as a secret chaos cult dedicated to Tsathogga the frog god. The cult is led by **Vermes**, a charismatic merchant who weaves many webs of mistrust in a bid to seize power in Sanctum and eventually conquer the entire region in the name of his dread lord.

Man-at-Arms: HD 1; **AC** 6 [13]; **Atk** spear (1d8) or short bow x2 (1d6); **Move** 12; **Save** 17; **AL** N; **CL/XP** 1/15; **Special:** none.
Equipment: ring mail, spear, short bow, 20 arrows.

Grubnitz: HD 1d4; **HP** 3; **AC** 9 [10]; **Atk** weapon (1d6); **Save** 18; **AL** N; **CL/XP** A/5; **Special:** none.

Vermes (Clr7): **HP** 23; **AC** 2 [17]; **Atk** +1 *light mace* (1d4+1); **Save** 9; **AL** C; **CL/XP** 8/800; **Special:** banish undead, +2 vs. poison and paralyzation, spells (2/2/2/1/1).
Spells: 1st— *cure light wounds, protection from good*; 2nd—*hold person x2*; 3rd—*prayer x2*; 4th—*cure serious wounds*; 5th—*finger of death.*
Equipment: plate mail, shield, +1 *light mace* (those hit with a natural '20' must save vs. *hold person* for 1d4+1 rounds), unholy symbol.

3714 Beached Riverboat

A fancy riverboat has been beached on the lakeshore, the crew sitting about scratching their heads while their captain sleeps off a snoot-full. The boat's passengers are either raging at the crew, sunning themselves, exploring the rocky shore under the watch of **four sailors** armed with spears and shields, or availing themselves of the liquor and card games aboard the ship. Prominent among the passengers are **three southmen** who are transporting a locked iron chest filled with a set of magic-user scrolls (*read magic, abacus eyes*, *detect treasure*) they are delivering to Old Wance in Sanctum, a grave Halayan bounty hunter called **Mazbury** (owns magnetic manacles that cannot be broken) and his prisoner, a Sanctumite smuggler called **Bonny Beph**, and the famed Sanctumite gambler **Mav**, in his characteristic finery milled in the far east.

Sailors: HD 1; **AC** 8 [11]; **Atk** spear (1d8); **Move** 12; **Save** 17; **AL** N; **CL/XP** 1/15; **Special:** none.
Equipment: shield, spear, 1d4sp.

Abacus Eyes

Spell Level: Magic-User, 2nd Level
Range: 10 feet
Duration: 1 round

This spell allows the caster to immediately total the value of all coins within 10 feet of him or her when the spell is cast.

Detect Treasure

Spell Level: Magic-User, 2nd Level
Range: 60 feet
Duration: 20 minutes

The caster can perceive, in places, people, or things, the presence of valuables or treasure. For example, hidden caches of coins, magic items, art objects, etc. can all be found with this spell.

Mazbury, Halayan (Ftr7): HP 26; **AC** 5 [14]; **Atk** +2 *man-catcher* (1 damage plus held, Open Doors roll to break free) or short sword (1d6) or throwing hammer (1d4); **Save** 8; **AL** L; **CL/XP** 7/600, **Special:** multiple attacks (7) vs. creatures with 1 or fewer HD.

> **Equipment:** chain mail, *+2 man-catcher*, short sword, throwing hammer, *magnetic manacles*; *+1 dagger* and *+1 ring of protection* (Mav's possessions).

Bonny Beph, Human Female (Thf5): HP 12; **AC** 7 [12]; **Atk** weapon (1d6); **Save** 11; **AL** N; **CL/XP** 5/240; **Special:** backstab (x3), +2 save vs. traps, read languages, thieving abilities.

> **Thieving Abilities:** Climb 89%, Tasks 35%, Hear 4 in 6, Hide 30%, Silent 40%, Locks 30%.
> **Equipment:** traveling clothes.

Mav (Thf8): HP 18; **AC** 6 [13]; **Atk** weapon (1d6); **Save** 9; **AL** C; **CL/XP** 8/800; **Special:** backstab (x3), +2 save vs. traps, read languages, thieving abilities.

> **Thieving Abilities:** Climb 92%, Tasks 50%, Hear 4 in 6, Hide 40%, Silent 50%, Locks 40%.
> **Equipment:** exotic clothing.

3717 Silver Canyon

This canyon is about 3 miles long and quite rugged. A small stream flows through the canyon and then disappears into a pool and seeps underground. The river sands are rich with arsenical silver. Each hour spent panning has a 1 in 6 chance of producing 1d10 silver pieces worth of silver, but the silver is mildly poisonous, robbing people of one point of constitution each day (saving throw negates) until they die.

3805 Mad Morva's Workshop

Mad Morva is an inventor with a rather chaotic (as in absent-minded and incredibly creative, not evil) mind. She lives in a cave complex that overlook Sanctum, where she works on her inventions and spells, aided by her three apprentices, **Orv**, **Yark** and **Trimble**, and her guard of **nine automatons**.

Her cave complex has been carved and refined into a mansion, with marble floors and wood panels in the foyer, hall and library. Her workshop is cluttered with ideas, most half-finished (or half-baked). There is a wide variety of tools and laboratory equipment, and a completed but non-activated iron golem in the form of a giant centipede hangs by chains from the ceiling, and there are three velocipedes (bicycles) in various stages of completion in one corner, being worked on by the apprentices.

Morva is hard to communicate with, but can be helpful if her interest is piqued. She has an eye for oddities and relics of the ancients, and would pay 10,000 for a creature she calls a prismati [04.20]. She'll even provide a magic bottle that, if uncorked in one's presence, will suck it in and hold it.

Orv, **Yark** and **Trimble (MU1):** HP 3, 2, 4; **AC** 9 [10]; **Atk** dagger (1d4) or staff (1d6); **Save** 15; **AL** N; **CL/XP** 1/15; **Special:** +2 vs. spells, spells (1).

> **Spells:** 1st—*magic missile.*
> **Equipment:** dagger or staff, spellbook.

Mad Morva, Human Female (MU9): HP 16; **AC** 8 [11]; **Atk** *+2 dagger* (1d4+2); **Save** 7; **AL** N; **CL/XP** 9/1100; **Special:** +2 vs. spells, spells (4/3/3/2/1).

> **Spells:** 1st—*charm person* x2, *magic missile* x2; 2nd—*phantasmal force* x3; 3rd—*dispel magic*, *hold person* x2; 4th—*charm monster*, *dimension door*; 5th—*teleport.*
> **Equipment:** *+2 dagger*, *+1 ring of protection*, spectacles (see through illusions and read people's alignments), spellbook.

Automaton: HD 1+1; **AC** 3 [16]; **Atk** heavy mace (1d8) or fists (1d4); **Move** 30; **Save** 17; **AL** L; **CL/XP** 2/30; **Special:** immune to disease and poison, resistance to electricity (50%).

New Monster Appendix

Batfolk

Hit Dice: 1
Armor Class: 9 [10]
Attacks: bite (1d6) or weapon
Saving Throw: 17
Special: none
Move: 12 (fly 21)
Alignment: Chaos
Number Appearing: 1, 2d20 or tribe of 10d10
Challenge Level/XP: 1/15

Batfolk are a race often found near mountains or areas with a number of natural caves. They are gregarious, usually found in large family groups, led by a priest or priestess. They live in caves, sometimes adding addtional structures within for privacy. Batfolk are tall and slender; averaging 7 feet tall and 150 lbs. Their wings look delicate, stretching translucent membrane 14 feet from wingtip to wingtip, but are actually tough and fast healing. Their favored choice of movement is gliding, but they can move quickly on the ground as well.

Batfolk: HD 1; AC 9 [10]; **Atk** bite (1d6) or weapon; **Save** 17; **Move** 12 (fly 21); **AL** C; **CL/XP** 1/15; **Special:** none.

Camelop

Hit Dice: 2+1
Armor Class: 7 [12]
Attacks: bite (1d3)
Saving Throw: 16
Special: none
Move: 20
Alignment: Neutrality
Number Appearing: 1 or 2d20
Challenge Level/XP: 2/30

Camelops are large camels, standing about 7 feet tall at the shoulder. They have small humps, and thus do not have quite the range of camels, but their greater carrying capacity makes them excellent pack animals.

Camelops: HD 2+1; AC 7 [12]; **Atk** bite (1d3); **Move** 20; **Save** 16; **AL** N; **CL/XP** 2/30; **Special:** none.

Century Worm

Hit Dice: 5
Armor Class: 7 [12]
Attacks: trample (2d4)
Saving Throw: 12
Special: none
Move: 9
Alignment: Neutrality
Number Appearing: 1, 1d10, or army of 10d10
Challenge Level/XP: 2/30

Century works are a large animal found in deserts, though they can tolerate a wide variety of habitat. Like the worm of their name, they do not have limbs, and propel themselves forward by bracing the back portion of their body while pushing and extending the front portion. Then the century worm drops the front portion of their body, straightens and pulls the back portion along. It is very like throwing themselves forward. They can achieve great speed, but the process is not very comfortable for their rider, leading to them generally being used as pack animals. Century worms attack by slamming their body against their assailant, then crushing them under the tough skin on their underside.

Century Worm: HD 5; **AC** 7 [12]; **Atk** trample (2d4); **Move** 9; **Save** 12; **AL** N; **CL/XP** 5/240; **Special:** none.

Fire Bees

Hit Dice: 3
Armor Class: 5 [14]
Attacks: sting (1d4 + 1d4 fire)
Saving Throw: 14
Special: immune to fire.
Move: 9 (fly 30)
Alignment: Neutrality
Number Appearing: 1, 1d4+1, or hive of 2d8+3
Challenge Level/XP: 4/60

Originally inhabitants of the elemental plane of Fire, fire bees can also be found near weak points between the plane of Fire and the Material Plane. These bees live in caves, often deep in the earth, generally near lava or in hot places. They fly out to gather nectar from crystal formations and large conflagrations in a process not well understood, and then create a hot spicy variety of honey.

Fire bees grow to approximately 6 feet in length, with a wingspan of about 8 feet. These creatures weigh 30 pounds and live in their adult form for 25–30 years. Fire bees' stingers can be used to sting foes repeatedly, with additional fire damage from their heat radiation.

Fire Bees: HD 3; AC 5 [14]; **Atk** sting (1d4 + 1d4 fire); **Move** 9 (fly 30); **Save** 14; **AL** N; **CL/XP** 4/60; **Special:** immune to fire.

Grimlock

Hit Dice: 2
Armor Class: 7 [12]
Attacks: weapon (1d8)
Saving Throw: 16
Special: can sense creatures and objects within 40 ft., immune to gaze attacks.
Move: 12
Alignment: Chaos
Number Appearing: 1d3+1, 1d4+4, 1d10+10, 1d6x10 plus 1 leader with 5HD per 10 adults
Challenge Level/XP: 2HD (4/60), 5 HD (7/600)

Grimlocks are evil and foul subterranean dwellers believed to be descendants of an ancient human race. Legends speak of long ago wars between various races that drove humans underground. For a while, they survived on what food they could forage, but eventually turned to cannibalism; beginning with small underground animals such as rats and other rodents, and eventually turning to aboveground raids on other races. Grimlocks dine on humanoid flesh and blood (with humans and dwarves being their favorite meals). They are primitive creatures, living in tribal communities of up to 60 or more individuals in underground caves and tunnels. Raiding and hunting bands often venture to the surface world to attack nearby settlements, capturing or killing those they encounter and returning to their lair to feast upon their spoils. Raids such as these are always conducted at night under the cover of darkness when grimlocks have the advantage. Grimlocks detest sunlight but are not harmed by it.

When not raiding the surface world, grimlocks often battle with other subterranean races including drow, dwarves, duergar, and even other grimlock tribes. Such battles can consist of outright warfare, but most of the time the battles are simple raids into other underground lairs to procure food (usually human or dwarven slaves kept by the other underground races). When engaged in wars with other races, grimlock leaders often ride basilisks into battle. Some larger grimlock lairs often have at least one medusa in midst as well.

A grimlock stands 5 to 6 feet tall and weighs 150 to 200 pounds. Its skin is slate gray and its hair is oily and matted. The creature emanates a stench that most others find nauseating, yet to a grimlock, it's a means of identification, for each scent is unique to a grimlock. Such fine distinctions are noticeable to other grimlocks, and possibly other creatures with a strong olfactory sense.

Due to their lack of sight, grimlocks prefer melee to ranged combat and close on enemies quickly when engaged. They attack with their menacing axes or powerful slams, slashing or pummeling their foes until their opponents are dead. Opponents that attempt to flee are run down and killed. Grimlocks that fall in combat are "honored" by being carried off the field of battle and devoured by their own.

Recent forays into underground caverns and caves by an intrepid band of adventurers speak of another race of grimlocks, civilized, and non-cannibalistic. These same adventurers speak of a large underground city full of these creatures. Whether these are truly advanced grimlocks or another race entirely is yet to be confirmed.

Grimlock: HD 2; AC 7 [12]; **Atk** weapon (1d8); **Move** 12; **Save** 16; **AL** C; **CL/XP** 2/30; **Special:** can sense creatures and objects within 40 ft., immune to gaze attacks.

Grimlock Leader: HD 5; AC 7 [12]; **Atk** weapon (1d8); **Move** 12; **Save** 12; **AL** C; **CL/XP** 7/600; **Special:** can sense creatures and objects within 40 ft., immune to gaze attacks.

Infant Vampire

Hit Dice: 1
Armor Class: 3 [16]
Attacks: bite (1d4 + sleep)
Saving Throw: 17
Special: drain level with hit, gaseous form, only killed in coffin, +1 or silver weapon to hit, regenerate (1hp/round).
Move: 6 (fly 9)
Alignment: Chaos
Number Appearing: 1, 1d4+1 or1d6+4
Challenge Level/XP: 4/60

An undead variant, infant vampires hatch from blood soaked eggs rather than being created from living humanoids. These creatures are quite rare, created under unusual circumstances. Generally, a spell casting vampire will encase a stillborn child in a caul-like substance that he or she creates, which then hardens as it preserves the body. Left near a source of negative energy, they infant vampires gradually incubates, waiting for the necessary blood to hatch.

Infant vampires are generally 2 feet long and weigh 10–12 lbs. Appearance is based on the original infant, with the addition of fangs, claw like fingers, and glowing red eyes. Infant vampires do not speak, though there are instances of longer lived examples understanding simple orders. Infant vampires do not grow into full adult vmpires; they are trapped in the infant stage for their entire existence. Infant vampires attack with their bite, which contains an anesthetic which causes sleep.

Infant Vampires: HD 1; AC 3 [16]; **Atk** bite (1d4 + sleep); **Move** 6 (fly 9); **Save** 17; **AL** C; **CL/XP** 4/60; **Special:** drain level with hit, gaseous form, only killed in coffin, +1 or silver weapon to hit, regenerate (1hp/round).

Kith-yin

Hit Dice: 4
Armor Class: 3 [16]
Attacks: silver sword (1d6+1)
Saving Throw: 13
Special: magical abilities (at will—ESP), psychic blast (1/day; save or suffer 1d4 points of intelligence damage and 1d6 points of hit point damage from pain, intelligence returns 1 point/day).
Move: 12
Alignment: Neutrality
Number Appearing: 1, 2d4 or 3d8
Challenge Level/XP: 5/240

Kith-yin look like emaciated elves (they are, in fact related, and are sometimes called astral elves). These creatures are commonly encountered on the Astral Plane.Kith-Yin live in extended family groups on their ships, sailing the Astral Plane in search of food, materiel, and slaves. A successful clan will have a variety of ships, with the best guarded housing noncombatants. Raiding ships, called hawks, range far and wide seeking valuables to return to the family.

Like their cousins, they are adept in the use of longsword and longbow, and their warriors often wield silver longswords. These are rumored to be able to banish travelers from the Astral Plane on a confirmed critical. Kith-Yin attack using weapons or spells, depending on their abilities. Raiding parties will often retreat if an attack goes badly. If the family ship is attacked, however, Kith-Yin fight to the death.

Kith-yin: HD 4; AC 3 [16]; **Atk** silver sword (1d6+1); **Move** 12; **Save** 13; **AL** N; **CL/XP** 5/240; **Special:** magical abilities (at will—ESP), psychic blast (1/day; save or suffer 1d4 points of intelligence damage and 1d6 points of hit point damage from pain, intelligence returns 1 point/day).
    Equipment: silver chain mail, silver longsword.

Nightgaunt

Hit Dice: 4
Armor Class: 5 [14]
Attacks: 2 claws (1d4) and tail (1d4 + submission)
Saving Throw: 13
Special: magic resistance (5%), submission (save or stunned for 1d4 rounds), surprise on 1–3 on 1d6.
Move: 12 (fly 21)
Alignment: Chaos
Number Appearing: 1or 1d4+1
Challenge Level/XP: 6/400

Nightgaunts are a race of night flying humanoids, often summoned for transport or to abduct persons for their summoner. They have an uncanny ability to traverse time and space, using routes unknown to other races. Nightgaunts can travel the spaces between planets safely for themselves and their passengers, making them a valuable though risky mode of transport. Nightgaunts stand 10 feet tall and have wings and tails. A nightgaunt has no discernible facial features, and horns rise from their head, where their brow should be. Their skin has an unpleasant rubbery texture, and they are hairless. The prehensile tail has a wicked stinger that cause targets to fall into a listless submission.

Nightgaunt: HD 4; AC 5 [14]; **Atk** 2 claws (1d4) and tail (1d4 + submission); **Move** 12 (fly 21); **Save** 13; **AL** C; **CL/XP** 6/400; **Special:** magic resistance (5%), submission (save or stunned for 1d4 rounds), surprise on 1–3 on 1d6.

Prismati

Hit Dice: 5
Armor Class: 1 [18]
Attacks: touch (2d4 cold, electricity or fire damage)
Saving Throw: 12
Special: magical abilities (1/day—*prismatic sphere*), +1 or better weapon to hit, resistance to cold, electricity and fire.
Move: 0 (fly 18)
Alignment: Neutrality
Number Appearing: 1, 1d4 or 3d6
Challenge Level/XP: 10/1400

Prismati are native to the astral plane, appearing as clouds of energy in shifting colors. These clouds produce a strange hum that becomes higher pitched when they are angry or upset, and takes on a low, throbbing rhythm when they are content. They are typically encountered on the material plane when travelling to or visiting a pilgrimage site of their, a well that emits prismatic energy. Communication, while possible, is difficult, given the alien nature of their speech. Due to their amorphous nature they are resistant to damage.

Prismati attack with their touch attack by brushing opponents and harming them with the energies of their form. If pressed, they use their *prismatic sphere* ability to gain time and the opportunity to flee.

Prismati: HD 5; AC 1 [18]; **Atk** touch (2d4 cold, electricity or fire damage); **Move** 0 (fly 18); **Save** 12; **AL** N; **CL/XP** 10/1400; **Special:** magical abilities (1/day—*prismatic sphere*), +1 or better weapon to hit, resistance to cold, electricity and fire.

Shimmering Radiance

Hit Dice: 8
Armor Class: 1 [18]
Attacks: touch (1d6)
Saving Throw: 8
Special: burn the flesh, +1 or better weapon to hit, wasting disease.
Move: 18
Alignment: Neutrality
Number Appearing: 1 or 1d10
Challenge Level/XP: 11/1700

A shimmering radiance is a strange entity that appears as a cloud of wispy smoke and shimmering motes of light. One can determine the "mood" of a shimmering radiance by the color – blue means anger, red depression and green joy. Their minds are quite alien, and thus their actions do not always fit their moods. A shimmering radiance is usually about 10 feet in diameter and roughly spherical. Their touch causes pronounced burns on the skin and can impart a wasting disease. In essence, they can make a single attack against any creature they have engulfed. Those struck by this disease must pass a saving throw each week or lose 1d4 points of constitution until the disease has been cured by magic. A shimmering radiance cannot run, and it can be moved about by strong winds, though usually in such conditions they cling close to the ground and, though they cannot attack, are also unmoved by the wind.

Shimmering Radiance: HD 8; AC 1 [18]; **Atk** touch (1d6); **Move** 18; **Save** 8; **AL** N; **CL/XP** 11/1700; **Special:** burn the flesh, +1 or better weapon to hit, wasting disease.

Silent Knight

Hit Dice: 7
Armor Class: 2 [17]
Attacks: weapon (1d8)
Saving Throw: 9
Special: silence (as *silence 15 ft radius*—constant).
Move: 9
Alignment: Neutrality
Number Appearing: 1 or 1d10
Challenge Level/XP: 11/1700

Silent Knights are an infernal golem-like creation, created to fight as foot soldiers in a never ending war against heaven. Forged of evil tainted metal, quenched in bile, silent knights gain the ability to move with unnatural stealth. Often, they are unnoticed until they strike. A silent knight stands 6 feet tall. They are humanoid in shape, forged entirely of lusterless black metal. Silent knights attack with whatever weapon was forged in their hands, most commonly a longsword.

Silent Knight: HD 7; AC 2 [17]; **Atk** weapon (1d8); **Move** 9; **Save** 9; **AL** N; **CL/XP** 8/800; **Special:** silence.

Snapping Dragonet

Hit Dice: 3
Armor Class: 2 [17]
Attacks: bite (2d6) or 2 claws (1d4)
Saving Throw: 14
Special: immune to sleep and charm, song, surprise on roll of 1–2 on 1d6 in desert environment.
Move: 9
Alignment: Neutrality
Number Appearing: 1 or 1d4+1
Challenge Level/XP: 4/120

Snapping dragonets are small dragons who burrow into the ground. They are nocturnal hunters, and not terribly intelligent. A snapping dragonet is about five ft. long. Their necks, backs and limbs are covered by thick, protective scales. These scales are usually patterned red and blue, but other colors have been seen. Most prized by hunters are the silver and white variety, which is quite uncommon, though spectacular in appearance. At night, they can sing a haunting song that often causes elves to fall into a deep reverie, essentially leaving them stunned for 1d6 hours. Snapping Dragonets attack with their claws and bite. They prefer to flee combat if at all possible if they do not initiate it.

Snapping Dragonet: HD 3; AC 2 [17]; **Atk** bite (2d6) or 2 claws (1d4); **Move** 12 (burrow 9); **Save** 14; **AL** N; **CL/XP** 4/120; **Special:** immune to sleep and charm, song, surprise on roll of 1–2 on 1d6 in desert environment.

Synthoid

Hit Dice: 2+2
Armor Class: 7 [12]
Attacks: fist (1d3)
Saving Throw: 16
Special: none.
Move: 12
Alignment: Neutrality
Number Appearing: 1 or 1d4+1
Challenge Level/XP: 2/30

Synthoids are a variant type of flesh golem. Often created for companionship, they are generally granted intelligence when they are created. Synthoids can have a variety of appearances, but are typically attractive and fit. Personality varies, but they are commonly friendly and companionable. A sythoid will usually try to avoid combat, but when pressed, will use its slam attack before trying to flee.

Synthoid: HD 2+2; AC 7 [12]; **Atk** fist (1d3); **Move** 12; **Save** 16; **AL** N; **CL/XP** 2/30; **Special:** none.

Varghoul

Hit Dice: 3
Armor Class: 5 [14]
Attacks: bite (1d6)
Saving Throw: 14
Special: disease (extra 1d6 points of damage), invisibility, undead.
Move: 24
Alignment: Chaos
Number Appearing: 1, 2 or 2d4
Challenge Level/XP: 5/240

Varghouls are undead wolves with ghoulish appetites. They are capable of becoming invisible for up to 6 rounds per day, and their bite injects toxins that cause one's flesh to flake off if they fail a saving throw. Varghouls attack in packs, harrying with their bite attack, bringing down prey. They only flee when more than half of a pack has been killed or incapacitated.

Varghoul: HD 3; AC 5 [14]; Atk bite (1d6); **Move** 24; **Save** 14; **AL** C; **CL/XP** 5/240; **Special:** disease (extra 1d6 points of damage), invisibility, undead.

Viper Hound

Hit Dice: 4
Armor Class: 4 [15]
Attacks: bite (1d4 + poison)
Saving Throw: 13
Special: lethal poison.
Move: 18
Alignment: Neutrality
Number Appearing: 1 or 2
Challenge Level/XP: 5/240

The viper hound looks like a large wolf with close-cropped, brownish-red fur and yellow eyes. They have pronounced fangs, like those of a cobra, and a poisonous bite. They are a solitary hunter, though once a pair mates, it is for life. Litters are typically 2–4 pups, able to hunt after about 8 weeks. Usually, the pups leave after a year, right before a new litter will be born. They can be trained a guard animal if acquired as a puppy. Generally the parents will defend a den to the death, so these puppies are rare and quite prized.

Viper Hound: HD 4; AC 4 [15]; Atk bite (1d4 + poison); **Move** 18; **Save** 13; **AL** N; **CL/XP** 5/240; **Special:** lethal poison.

Walking Slime

Hit Dice: 5
Armor Class: 9 [11]
Attacks: touch (1d6 + turn to slime)
Saving Throw: 12
Special: cast spells as 5th level druid (3/2/1), transform to slime.
Move: 6
Alignment: Neutrality
Number Appearing: 1 or 2d4
Challenge Level/XP: 8/800

Walking slimes are a race that is rumored to have been created in some horrific arcane experiment. While they appear to be humanoid, and are quite intelligent, closer examination yields the fact that they are actually slime held together in a humanoid form. Powerful druids are not uncommon. While there is speculation on how they can retain their humanoid shape, there have only been a few who encountered them who escaped. Those who have say that they can shift between slime and humanoid forms with ease.

Walking Slime: HD 5; AC 9 [11]; **Atk** touch (1d6 + turn to slime); **Move** 6; **Save** 12; **AL** N; **CL/XP** 8/800; **Special:** cast spells as 5th level druid (3/2/1), transform to slime.
    Spells: 1st—*faerie fire x3*; 2nd—*heat metal, produce flame*; 3rd—*protection against fire*.